INVISIBLE

IN A SMALL TOWN

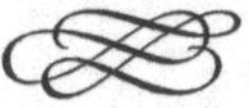

ALIE GARNETT

<h1 style="text-align:center">CHAPTER 1</h1>

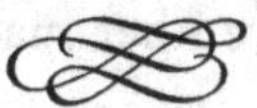

The desk was hard against her bare back, but Jessa wasn't noticing. All her attention was on Jack and what his hands were doing to her overheated, wet body. Every touch was making her body quiver in anticipation. Her breath hitched as Jack's skilled hand unclasped her lacy black bra, leaving her breasts bare for his piercing brown gaze alone.

"Jessa, you are gorgeous," Jack's gravelly voice hissed as he ran a thumb over her pert nipple, causing her to moan his name.

"Anderson, please, make me yours," Jessa whispered, but he seemed to already know exactly what she wanted, needed, as his mouth descended...

GROANING, Ruth Kennedy stopped typing to delete out Anderson and replace the name with Jack's again. It had been happening since she began writing the book. This time just solidified that she needed to change Jack's name to something better. Of course, not Anderson, because Jack could never be Anderson.

Anderson. Even seeing his name on her screen broke her concentration. Her mind had been on nothing but Jessa and Jack and their romance for hours. That was until Anderson entered the scene, and of course, it had to be during a hot sex scene. Some, if not all, of that was Ruth's own fault. In her mind, that scene had happened in Anderson's office. Her boss's office!

The classic country quickly faded away as she pulled out her headphones. She needed them to block out the world, and they were necessary to her writing processes. Well, not the whole world, but the noise of the computer equipment that surrounded her. The whirling and beeping would have driven her mad if she had no way to block it out.

Stretching, she looked around the almost completely dark room before flipping the light switch she had under her desk. Getting up from her desk was something she just did not want to do all the time, so she had installed the switch years before. Instantly, her work apartment was bathed in bright light. It was a smaller apartment with an old couch with a white sheet covering the awful orange color and two large desks creating a large U shape that held all her equipment.

With a mouse click, she saved her work on the screen. It was the biggest she could find. On the opposite desk behind her was a slightly older and smaller version of her computer, and it was hooked up to more networking equipment than Ruth thought was possible. Unfortunately, it was all needed. That internet equipment made it possible to store the programs in a way that she could access them from anywhere in the building at any time. It was a must-have so that she could work from anywhere in the building, and that included the office she had borrowed for the half-written scene.

Since she lived and worked in the building, being able to access her files at any moment was important. Her day job as a personal assistant in an insurance office gave structure to her life that she would lose if she only wrote her books. Writing could be all-consuming for her if she let it, so she stayed working, even if it cut into her writing time.

Getting up, she realized it was way past midnight, and if she had any hope of sleeping that night, she needed to do it now. She'd had many nights like this where she didn't sleep but instead worked until she nearly passed out from fatigue on the couch in the corner of the room. It was the only reason she'd kept it over the years.

Going across the hall, she turned the lights on and off as she moved. She closed the door to her office and walked into the larger apartment that had been her home for over ten years. Maybe she had no yard, and sometimes there was loud traffic that came through from the street below, but there were downfalls to owning a traditional house too. So far, she hadn't gotten tired of living downtown and couldn't see that happening anytime soon.

She had started working for Frank Berg in the office downstairs just out of high school. There had been no reason for her to go to college at that time. Her plan was already set. She was going to marry her high school sweetheart and have a dozen kids. Maybe not a dozen, but more than two that was for sure. So, she had started working for Frank since he was her future father-in-law, and it was the business they would eventually take over. Everything she did was for the future they would share.

The man she'd loved and had put all her hopes and dreams into, Franky Berg, would go to college and get his degree. She was to stay back in Landstad and save money for their home, a family, etc. So, she did just that.

They had moved into the apartment together the summer after graduation. Since that day, she had made it her home—even after Franky had decided he no longer wanted her. She had stayed, and now ten years later, she barely remembered him being there.

Pouring herself a glass of water before she went to bed, she went to the front window to see what was happening in the little town she called her own. Landstad, North Dakota might be a small dot on the map, but it had its lively moments. And once in a while, she got to watch them from her window.

Two blocks down, The Landing still had a fair number of cars and trucks parked near it, which meant that it was still open. As the only bar in town, it usually had a brisk business, just not on the weekends since that was when the locals could venture out of their one-bar town to drink in more populated places.

But tonight was the start of a three-day blizzard, which meant everyone would be keeping close to home. There was already more snow in the street than there had been at five when the insurance office had closed, and she had walked the twenty feet to her front door.

The wind was already blowing the snow around and making drifts wherever it could. The weatherman had promised the storm would be a bad one, but the weathermen around here were known to get it wrong sometimes. This time it seemed they had been right.

Still holding her glass in hand, she noticed her neighbor from across the street shoveling out her car. The drifts were almost knee-high, and she was struggling. Ruth knew she would be of little help with the task but felt guilty just watching her. It was cold, and she probably needed to be some place.

Ruth knew the woman was Amanda Nordskov, and she was the new nurse practitioner in town. She was a tiger—a nickname used for those who graduated from Landstad High School and never seemed to leave. Otherwise, tigers would come back when they realized life was better here.

Amanda had been a few years ahead of her in school, and Ruth really didn't know her well, but she could pick her out of a crowd. That's how small towns were. Ruth did know Amanda's younger sisters, Kit and Julia. Kit had graduated the same year as Ruth, and Julia had been a year younger. Both had been popular, something Ruth had never been. But when you went to school with someone for twelve years, you considered them your friends, even if you barely spoke to them most of the time.

Deciding nobody else was going to help the woman, Ruth headed for the door, leaving her glass on the counter. Since she owned the building and both apartments, she had taken to keeping her outer-wear in the hallway. Quickly, she stuffed her bare feet into her boots and pulled on a white hat over her blonde hair. She didn't take time to put it up, just letting it hang around her shoulders.

After grabbing her thick mittens, she headed for the door. She was sure that by the time she made it to the car, someone else would have shown up. That was how it usually worked. Since she wasn't going to spend a lot of time in the snowstorm and was wearing an oversized sweatshirt and another layer below it, she felt she would be fine.

Once out the door, the wind instantly blew through her shirt, and she realized it was cold. But she headed across the street anyway, not thinking the chore was going to take long. Though, nobody else had shown up yet.

"Need help?" she asked as Amanda tossed another shovel of snow into the street from behind her car.

"Yes!" She sounded relieved as she looked up with a smile. "Get in the car and see if you can drive, and I will push. I needed to be at the nursing home an hour ago."

"Okay," she said and Ruth jumped into the driver's seat of the already running and thankfully warm car. This was the reason she didn't have a car. It was easier to have her mom drive her places. It may not be convenient, but it was easier during the winter months then digging it out of a snow bank.

After putting the car in gear, she gently hit the gas and felt the car move forward about an inch before the wheels just spun. Whether Amanda was pushing or not, Ruth didn't know.

Ruth tried every trick in the book to get the car out of the snow-bank. She was sure it needed more than she could provide; her skills in winter driving were lacking. Which was exactly why she usually didn't volunteer to help.

Getting out, she looked over at Amanda, who was still trying to push the car out. Despite it being in park.

"I think it's stuck." Ruth rubbed her gloved hands over her chilled arms.

"Don't say that!" Amanda groaned and stopped trying to push. Just then, a cop car pulled up with its lights flashing but no siren. Amanda turned and looked at the car and cursed. *Loudly.*

The cruiser stopped in the middle of the street because in Land-stad, you can, and the door opened, revealing a tall, handsome cop. His bulky jacket and winter hat didn't hide who he was. Hue Strong had been a cop in town a number of years and had grown up here.

"Need help, ladies?" he asked, but he was only looking at Amanda.

"Hue, I need a ride to the nursing home." Amanda seemed to have gotten over her anger at the cop being there.

"This isn't a taxi service, Nordskov," Hue stated, though he was smiling, and Ruth was one hundred percent sure he would give her a ride.

"You're basically a glorified traffic cop, Strong. I am going to guarantee that nobody is going to speed through town tonight." Amanda grabbed her bag from the back seat of the car. "Ruth, can you turn off my car and run my keys to my apartment? Hubert here will be driving me around tonight."

Hue shook his head but went around the cruiser and opened the door for her. As she got into the car, he stated, "Don't call me Hubert." Then he slammed the door on Amanda and headed around the car. "Night, Ruth."

"Goodnight, Hue," she said with a smile, seeing the sexual tension behind their banter. Romance was her jam, after all.

Doing as Amanda instructed, she shut off the car and locked it, even if she was sure Amanda never did. Few doors were locked in this town, home, or vehicle. Sure, they had crime, but they mostly knew who was committing the crime.

Up the stairs, she found Amanda's apartment unlocked and set the keys on her table. Looking around, she didn't really notice much about this apartment, not the worn carpet or the faded paint. All if which she left up to the tenant to change if they wanted. It was one thing she knew most owners didn't allow but she wanted her tenants to make their apartments their home. Not that anyone actually knew that since she used a rental agency so that nobody who rented from her actually knew she was the owner.

Leaving Amanda's apartment, she went down the stairs and back out into the blizzard, only this time it was just to get home. Now that she had nothing keeping her, she was in a hurry. It was freezing after all, and she had regretted not taking a jacket since stepping foot out the door.

She had expected to hit a wall of cold, not a wall of man. She instantly barreled right into someone walking down the sidewalk, a sidewalk in North Dakota in the dark in the middle of a blizzard that should be completely empty.

Unable to get her balance back with the slippery snow under her feet, she could feel she was going to fall into the snowbank that Amanda had only made larger with her snow shovel. As she fell, she held tight to the man's bulky jacket. Her body hit the snow, and he landed on top of her in a pile of arms and legs and a very distinct cologne.

Her eyes instantly searched his face and found the answer: Anderson. Her very own, very sexy, very drunk boss was pressing her body into a snowbank. Between the freezing cold on her back and his head on hers, she was instantly too confused to even think. Not that she wanted to.

His hands were around her waist and had slipped under her sweatshirt in the fall. She quietly cursed the layer of thermal shirt that blocked his fingers from touching skin. This was her every fantasy come true, and she was wearing too much clothing.

His eyes found hers, and he gave her a small smile as the snow fell around them and the wind whipped at their clothes. Time stopped when she thought he was going to kiss her. All she could do was watch his mouth as it descended towards hers.

Was this really happening, or had her imagination gotten away from her? Again!

CHAPTER 2

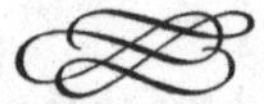

How drunk was he? Because one minute Anderson Miles was walking down the sidewalk, and the next, he was hit by an angel. It wasn't even Christmas!

She was soft and warm, completely covered in white, and falling from the sky. Because one moment he was alone, and the next, she was in his arms.

Looking at her in the streetlight glow with her nearly white blonde hair spread over the white snow, she looked like the angel he was sure she was. Her eyes opened, and he was looking into icy blue depths that instantly captivated him. He leaned closer to her, and her gaze shifted to look at his mouth.

Who was this woman, and where the hell had she come from? Had fate sent her?

Not an hour before, he had just told his friend Rafferty at the bar that this town wasn't the kind of place he was going to find love. But suddenly, he was rethinking that. Maybe there was someone in this town worth staying for.

"Sorry," he mumbled, then stopped staring at her and started to get up, or tried to. All he seemed able to do was roll off her into the snow pile beside her. Closing his eyes, he rubbed his face, still seeing those ice-blue eyes. With some effort, he sat up and explained, "I think I might have drank too much."

When she didn't say anything, he opened his eyes and looked at the snowbank beside him, but it was empty. She was gone. He looked up and down the sidewalk but didn't see her or any sign of her. She had vanished, and all that was left of her was an indent in the snow pile.

Flopping back into the cold snow, he stared at the falling snowflakes and wondered if she had just been a figment of his imagination. *Was she even real? Was he drunk enough to hallucinate?*

"Are you passed out, Anderson?" Rafferty Brooks kicked his foot, causing him to sit up.

A few weeks ago, he had gone out for a drink at the only bar in town and had stumbled into Rafferty. They had been hanging out since then. Anderson liked Rafferty, he was a fun guy who knew everyone in town. But then again, the man had been raised here, whereas Anderson had just moved here four years before.

Until recently, Anderson had always driven the hour and a half from Landstad to spend every weekend with his girlfriend, Daphne. He and Daphne had been dating and living together on the weekends for almost five years. In that time, he had twice asked her to marry him, and almost every month or so, they would talk about her moving to Landstad. None of those things had happened because she had a career in real estate that she was not giving up to live with him in some back-water town up north.

Even so, late last fall, when he had asked her again to marry him, he wanted more than her weekends. It wasn't the first time, but he was sure she was in the same place as he was. After all, it had been five years. Instead, she had actually laughed at him, callously informing him that his brother had proposed not three days before and that she had accepted his proposal. The better proposal.

Anderson had been devastated, not just by her words but by her attitude. Numb and hollow, he had walked out of the restaurant they were in, leaving her behind to figure out her own way home. After packing his stuff as best he could, he headed home to Landstad. After that, he had only been back but once or twice for holidays.

In hindsight, he could see now that he hadn't really loved Daphne. It had just been time to settle down, and she had been in his life. His brother Jonathan would not marry her because he was already married to an amazing woman with two kids. He was just trying to take what Anderson had—that was how Jonathan had always been. In the end, his brother cheating on his wife was what had pissed Anderson off more than him taking Daphne. His brother's wife deserved better.

"Do you believe in angels?" he asked, his mind back on the woman he had just had in his arms. He could still feel her against him.

"I'll drive you home, buddy. I can tell weekends in Landstad are a little too much for you." Rafferty laughed and grabbed his hand, pulling him to his feet.

Anderson waved him off and replied, "I think an angel landed on me."

Anderson half hoped that Rafferty had an explanation for what had happened, that maybe he had seen it happen and could either tell him he was drunk or who he had run into. Anderson was sure she had been a real woman, all curves and softness and vanilla-scented.

Rafferty ignored him. "We can do lunch, and you can pick up your truck when you're sober again."

"I think she was a real woman," Anderson admitted, now convinced that she was real. She was just able to disappear, like a superpower...so maybe not so real.

"Sure, buddy, we all do." He chuckled and slapped Anderson on the back, then pushed him towards his truck.

Anderson went willingly because, after all that, he was sure that she was real. Or maybe he was too drunk to even know since she had vanished as fast as she had appeared.

* * *

Hours later, Anderson was back on Main Street in Landstad, about to throw up in the middle of a 50s style café. Rafferty had picked him up for the promised lunch, and they were at Mia's, one of only two restaurants in town. This one was by far the most popular with the locals.

Not that Anderson could blame them—the place was quaint and charming and looked the exact same as it had four years before when he had first seen it. It was right out of 1955, and the charm of it was never lost on him. Even today, when he was sick enough to throw up, the café still maintained its charm.

"How can you eat that?" Anderson watched him eat and tried not to gag at the mere smell.

"How can you not?" Rafferty replied as he just kept shoveling more of the greasy eggs in his mouth before digging into his hash browns.

The café door opened, letting in a cold blast of air, and everyone in the café looked to see who'd walked in. The chilled air actually helped to settle his rolling stomach. People-watching was more than a hobby in a small-town café; it was a sport. Knowing what everyone else was doing was just what everyone did.

The wind had blown in a tall blonde in a thick blue jacket and white boots. Not able to look away, he watched her gloved hands as she pushed off the snow that had settled on her. Her long hair was completely covering her face, still disheveled from the wind. Instantly, he knew he was looking at his angel again. The woman who had appeared out of nowhere last night had just walked into the cafe.

She was real, and now he was in the same room as her. The more he looked at her, the more he felt like he had met her before. After living in Landstad for over four years, he knew quite a few of its residents, but not all by any means. Something about her just seemed familiar.

The woman turned away from him and pulled off her gloves and jacket, revealing a soft cream-colored, form-fitting sweater underneath. Curves that the sweater accentuated were further highlighted by the tight jeans she wore—jeans that did great things to her back end. She pulled her hair back from her face as she turned back towards the room with a smile. Because in a town this size, she was sure to know everyone there.

As she ran her fingers through her hair, Anderson's breath caught in his throat. Ruth Kennedy. *No*, he decided, *it couldn't be*. Ruth Kennedy wore her white-blonde hair in a bun on the top of her head every day. Ruth Kennedy was at least ten years older than this woman, this angel. Maybe she was a sister, a gorgeous sister that he'd never met.

Ruth Kennedy was his personal assistant, and he saw her nearly every day. Not that he knew much about the woman who kept his office running smoothly, but he should have known about a sister. A sister would have stopped by the office at least once in four years.

Her ice-blue eyes caught him staring, and she stared back at him. They were the same eyes he looked into last night. Her smile remained as she walked towards them as if she hadn't run him down the night before, but then it suddenly vanished.

How had he not realized who she was the night before? She was so much a part of his life that he had stopped noticing her long ago. She was his personal assistant, nothing more. He couldn't be suddenly attracted to his assistant. It had to be a sister.

"Hello, Anderson. Awful weather today," she said, just like she did the morning before at the office when the snow had started to fall. His hopes of a sexy sister were dashed. It was just her. Still sexy, but in a works-for-him way.

Anderson found himself unable to breathe. What had happened to his prickly, quiet personal assistant? On the weekends, she was a gorgeous white-haired angel, and he had never known it. Going home every weekend had made him miss a lot around town. Ruth was a changed woman when he had been gone. Everything had changed about her, from her white hair down to the white winter boots on her feet, none of which he had ever seen on her before.

"Ruth," he managed to reply, hoping she would say she was not Ruth. Ruth couldn't possibly look this good on the weekends; she wore a blouse and skirt every day. It was like she had a uniform she had to wear. There was no way she could be so different in and out of the office.

Then there was the run-in. Had she completely forgotten, or had he imagined the entire thing? Maybe it had been a dream, one with someone he knew in a completely new way, a sexy way. He could almost convince himself it was a dream if it wasn't for the eyes. He hadn't noticed those eyes before, and now he couldn't look away.

Those gorgeous eyes turned from him to his lunch companion. Her usual pale face went paler when she saw Rafferty there. Was it because Rafferty also sold insurance? They should be enemies, but they were actually good friends. Their jobs had never been an issue for them, nor did they ever talk about work or being competitors.

Rafferty looked up at Ruth and flashed her his usual cocky smile, the one that always got the ladies to smile back at him. "Angel."

Instantly, Anderson turned away from the woman and stared at his friend. What had he just called her? Had he actually called her Angel? Had he made the connection?

Ruth's reaction was to huff and storm off further into the restaurant beyond him. All he wanted to do was turn and look at her again, but he didn't want it to seem obvious that he was watching her. So, when she was out of his view, all he could see was Rafferty, who was chuckling as he took another bite of eggs.

The purple-haired waitress walked up to the table and glared down at Rafferty. When he finally looked up, she scolded him. "Leave her alone, Brooks."

Despite her odd hair color, she was the owner of the place and had been since he had first met her. Over the years, Mia's hair had been every color of the rainbow. Well, every color except for the actual color hair comes in. It had taken some getting used to, but now he couldn't see her in normal hair. She was known for her hair and her knowledge of everything and everyone in this town. All of it. On top of that, she knew every inch of the town's history, all the way back to its founding.

"Who?" Rafferty acted all innocent with his question, his eyes looking the woman up and down as she stood there, not even trying to hide his interest in her.

"Don't be all flirty with me. It does not work. Never has." She walked away, tired of her conversation with them. Everyone in town knew that the two did not get along and never had. On more than one occasion, Rafferty had been banned from the cafe. It seemed he was starting down that road again.

"Oh, it has worked, Mia," he called after her, not caring that people were listening.

Anderson watched him go back to eating again, chuckling to himself. Rafferty never had a problem finding women. Most loved him, but it seems there were two here today who did not, though it didn't seem to bother the man one bit.

"I don't think she likes you very much," Anderson teased his friend.

"Which one? Mia, who wants me badly, or Angel, who needs her feathers ruffled sometimes before she ends up like her mom?" Rafferty questioned, his eyes shooting back towards the kitchen where Mia had disappeared into.

"Angel. Why did you call Ruth that?"

"Ruth?" Rafferty seemed confused for a moment, but then realization dawned with a smile. "We used to call her 'Angel' in school. We graduated together."

"Why?" Anderson suddenly wanted to know everything about the woman he had worked with for years.

"Because we are the same age," Rafferty stated. She seemed older than Rafferty, but Rafferty didn't seem exactly grown up.

Anderson shook his head at the man. "No, why the nickname?"

Rafferty rolled his eyes at his friend. "Did you not see her at all? That hair has always been that color. White like an angel's. She didn't act like it back then, though. Quite the troublemaker, she was."

Anderson couldn't imagine Ruth as a kid; she always acted more mature and professional. But it seemed Ruth was younger than he was. Since he'd met her, he had thought she was at least forty but oddly looked the exact same as she had when he first came to town, not aging at all. It must have been her clothes that had made him think she was older because today, for the first time, she looked as young as she actually was.

"I don't see her as a troublemaker."

Mild-mannered, always-on-task Ruth. As far as he could tell, she had never done anything that even came close to getting into trouble. Even the woman out in the middle of a snowstorm didn't seem like she was trouble.

"It was probably more Franky than Angel, I suppose. They were always getting caught being horny teenagers, and they must have started dating at around twelve." Rafferty finally finished his eggs, to Anderson's relief.

"Where is Franky now?" He could imagine seeing this new Ruth making out with a boyfriend, but the office-Ruth was harder to picture doing something like that.

"I don't know. Wherever Frank Berg ended up. I think he moved to be closer to Franky and his family. He ended up being a jerk. Franky, not Frank. Frank was great letting her work over there for years, and then he made you hire her. He took care of her, and I respect him for that. Angel deserves everything she gets." Rafferty looked past Anderson to where she must've been sitting. It seemed his buddy had a soft spot for the woman despite her feelings for him.

Frank Berg had been the man Anderson's company had bought the insurance office from four years before. He had worked in Landstad for over thirty years when he retired, though as far as Anderson knew, he hadn't returned, leaving his entire past behind when he left.

"So, you don't hate her; she just hates you?" Anderson questioned, trying to get a handle on the relationship between the two.

"Yup, can't blame her, though. I wish we could be friends. She was fun in the old days." Rafferty once again looked in the direction she must've been sitting.

"Friends or *friends*?" Anderson said with an eyebrow raised, wishing he had chosen that side when they had come in earlier. He wanted another look at the woman, even if he could look at her all day, every day at work. Today was different.

"Gross, man. We're related," Rafferty said as Mia walked by with a tray of dirty dishes.

Anderson watched his friend reach out and slap the woman hard on her butt. She just kept going with her tray, not letting it get to her. Anderson watched Rafferty laugh, except within seconds, the woman was back, trayless, and had Rafferty's head pushed into the window at the end of the booth.

She slammed it into the window again when she said, "If you ever touch me again, Rafferty Brooks, I will kill you. And you know that isn't an empty threat. Nobody would even find your body." She then yanked his hat off his head. With force, she threw it on the floor and walked away from the booth again.

Anderson was laughing when Rafferty sat up, his hair a complete mess. The previous cheerful attitude was gone. Straightening his hair as best he could, he finally gave a brittle smile as he said, "God, she wants me."

"I think you are delusional, man," Anderson said as he got up, throwing a twenty-dollar bill on the table. He wasn't eating, and Rafferty was probably going to be kicked out of the cafe again.

"Nope. That, my friend, is Mia. She's a feisty one." Rafferty followed him and got up, adding his own money to the table. Zipping up their jackets, they walked out into the blowing snow. North Dakota winter storms were legendary, and this one was going to be a good one.

They waved goodbye, and Anderson climbed into his cold pickup. He quickly started it and waited for it to warm up a little. As he sat there, the café door opened, and two women came out: Tess Thorn from the bank and Ruth in her blue coat, zipped to her chin. Once the wind hit them, her white hair went flying everywhere. She was living up to the image in his mind of an angel.

Putting the car in gear, he pulled away from the curb as they walked by, neither of them looking his way. They seemed very different, and he wondered if they were friends. But then again, he was beginning to think he had no idea who Ruth really was. Based on what Rafferty had said, they were close to the same age. That made the woman around thirty and younger than Anderson was. He had to admit it was the hair that had made him think she was older. White hair on a twenty-something was odd, but in his defense, she always acted and dressed older than she was.

Nothing had ever pointed him in the direction of a troublemaking young woman. He would have to see if there was any of that left in her, see if she was still the angel she had been in high school.

CHAPTER 3

Ignore, *ignore*, she demanded herself as she walked away from Anderson and his friend, Rafferty, a friend who should be an enemy. Enemies made more sense since they were in competing offices. There were only so many people needing insurance around here. Mortal enemies would've been perfect!

Eyes trained ahead of her, she focused on Tess Thorn, Landstad Bank's first female president. Once again, she wished that they had met anywhere other than Mia's Cafe in the middle of Landstad. The last thing she needed was to be gossiped about. Except with the storm, they had little choice if they wanted to meet in person.

A few days before, they had met online late in the evening when Ruth had been looking through Facebook and a post caught her eye. It asked if anyone had read the book about Ted Bundy that had just come out. Quickly, she responded since she had read it the previous weekend at her moms, and when she hit 'send,' the post vanished, which made her nervous. After all, the post had been about a murderer. But the person had messaged her, and they had messaged back and forth for a few hours about the book and others they had also read. Then Tess had asked if she wanted to meet with the possibility of forming some sort of book club.

Today had been that day. Since they both lived and worked in a town of fewer than two thousand people, they had agreed to meet at the cafe. They had never spoken until today, despite being next-door neighbors for over a year. But then again, it wasn't like they had lawns or reasons to hang out at their front doors.

Looking up and seeing Tess Thorn, she hurried over to her booth and slid in across from her. Not looking back to see what either man was doing, she looked at the woman sitting across from her. Over the last year, she had seen the blonde bank president around town. She may run the bank Ruth kept her money in, but Ruth had no reason to talk to the president, ever. When she had needed a loan she went elsewhere, bypassing the local gossip when a loan was actually needed. In reality, she hadn't had one of those since this woman came to town.

Seeing her up close, Ruth noticed that the woman was younger than she had thought she would be. Being a president, Ruth had expected her to be a decade or more older. The woman couldn't have been more than forty. Wavy hair just touching her shoulders made her look every inch the professional she was. Her light gray eyes were a surprise—very unusual. She made a mental note about that for a character later.

Tess stuck out her hand with a professional smile. "Tess Thorn."

Smiling, Ruth took her hand. "Ruth Kennedy."

The awkwardness was broken when the waitress came to their table and dropped off two waters and menus in a flurry, "Here are the menus. Hey, Ruth, not at your mom's today?"

Ruth looked up at the waitress. Of course, Mia knew everyone's business—that was her business. Once again, hating some aspects of small-town life, gossip being a big one, she fake smiled. "No, no, it's storming, so I am staying in town."

"I suppose, wouldn't want Chester to have to drive in snow." The waitress looked out the window at the stormy street.

Everyone knew that Ruth's parents were Sara and Chester Kennedy and that on weekends, she went to their place. And she got a ride there. It wasn't that she couldn't drive; it was just easier not to sometimes. Winters were those times.

"Mia," Ruth warned. She had known Mia Lawson almost her entire life. Both of them had been raised in town, and neither had yet to leave it. And in all that time, Ruth had not become friends with Mia…for obvious reasons.

"Sorry, there's just a little tension in here right now," Mia stated cryptically, looking around the room. The action made her purple ponytail flop around.

"You and Rafferty now, and Natalie Beckett and Hazel May are here. I don't think either one knows. Yet." Mia walked away, as her name was called by a man in the back.

Tess watched as the waitress walked away. Turning back to Ruth, she asked, "You and Rafferty Brooks?"

Of course, Tess would already know who Rafferty was. That and Rafferty always made a point of knowing the women in town, new or old. He knew them all.

"Not like that. Ick. He is just a jerk; always has been." Ruth tried to stem the gossip on that immediately. Even the thought had given her a shudder of mild disgust.

"You could do worse," Tess said with a shrug.

"*Ick,*" Ruth emphasized the word a bit louder.

"So, what did you think of the book?" Tess asked, returning them to the topic that brought them there.

"What did you think about it?" Ruth did not want to tell her opinion first in case Tess thought otherwise. What if their completely different opinions destroyed whatever friendship they might have? Then what?

"What book?" Mia was back with her pad for their orders.

"You would not be interested," Ruth hissed, hoping Tess would take the hint and not tell Mia anything.

"The new one on Ted Bundy," Tess answered at the same time, missing the hint.

"I think the author had a major thing for him. It was kind of creepy." Mia had an opinion about everything and would share it with anyone.

"You read it?" Ruth asked in shock. She and Mia had nothing in common. There was no way they would have a shared reading preference.

"I thought that too," Tess said and then added that she wanted the salad.

"I read a different one a few years ago that was way better on him," Mia said, not asking Ruth what she wanted as she scribbled their order in her notepad, which Ruth didn't care about because Mia knew she wanted the special. She always ordered the same thing. Before Ruth could say anything about it, Mia was called away by a customer.

"If we create a book club, maybe we could invite her, too. She has read more than one book on Ted Bundy. I think she would be interested," Tess said.

"No, not Mia," Ruth replied. Mia is a year younger than her and was a bubbly cheerleader, popular, and loved to have a good time. Completely the opposite of Ruth. Even though her cheerleading days were ten years behind her, that was still how Ruth saw her. Pasts were hard to get over in a small town.

"Why?" Tess asked as the woman in question slid their plates onto the table with a smile and no time to stop as she hurried away.

When she was gone, Ruth whispered, "Mia is Mia."

"Maybe you guys could bond over serial killers and your dislike of Rafferty Brooks. Looks like she has no time for Mr. Flirty," Tess said as she watched Mia.

Turning, she looked and caught Mia grab his knit hat and throw it on the ground, only to stomp on it as she went back into the kitchen, catching sight of the back of Anderson's head as he got a front-row seat to the exchange. Maybe she would ask him on Monday about it, but she would probably chicken out.

"I guess you can. I am not," Ruth stated, unwrapping her silverware.

When Mia finally made it back to their table, Tess asked Mia if she was interested in a book club. Ruth's hopes were dashed when Mia seemed excited about the idea. The time and place were set by Mia herself: tomorrow right here. Leave it to her to take over the entire thing within seconds of being invited.

Mia returned to work, and the other two went to pay for their meals. Ruth walked to the resister at the café's front, noticing Anderson and Rafferty had both left. Their plates were still on the table, but the men were gone.

Bills paid, they both grabbed their jackets from the rack by the door, then headed out the door into the blowing, swirling snowstorm. At least the walk was short.

As she walked down the street beside Tess Thorn, Ruth wondered what the woman thought of the storm. She wasn't actually from the area, so maybe she didn't have an appreciation for it like Ruth did. Stopping in front of the insurance office, she said to Tess, "This is me."

"Are you going to work?" Tess looked puzzled as she tried to keep her own hair from flying in the wind.

Ruth laughed. "No, I live above it. Short commute that way."

"Then you are my neighbor! I live right there." Tess pointed at the next building. It was a drug store on the main floor with three apartments above it.

"Yes, we are," Ruth said, trying not to sound like she already knew that. She knew everything about downtown. Not much happened that she didn't know about. It was her neighborhood, after all.

Last year when Tess had moved to town, Ruth had watched her move her boxes from her window next door. Thinking back on it, she should have helped but hadn't felt like it that day. Now she wished she had; they might have a lot in common. They might have been friends before this.

"See you tomorrow then?" Tess asked, sounding as unsure as Ruth felt about it.

"Yes. At three at the cafe again," Ruth agreed and hurried through the door into the warmth. She didn't do well with small talk.

After parting, she went up to her apartment, shrugged off her heavy navy jacket, and hung it on a hook in the hallway. Then she pulled off her boots and left them out there also. Slipping on her cozy slippers, she walked into the apartment that faced Main Street. Two bedrooms, two bathrooms of all Ruth. She walked to the window to see if she could see Tess walk into her place but knew it wouldn't have taken the woman that long to make it a few feet to her door, especially in the blowing snow and cold.

With Tess gone, her eyes went to the spot she had fallen into with Anderson. After a night and morning of more snow, she couldn't even tell which snow pile it was. Now that Amanda's car was shoveled out and gone from the street, all evidence had been erased.

Turning from the window, she smiled. The Saturday storm meant she finally had a day for herself. Usually, her mother or stepfather, Chester, would come and get her as the workday ended on Friday, and she stayed at their farm twelve miles from town until church on Sunday. They would then drop her off at her apartment, or she sometimes walked home from church in the summer. Over the years, it was just easier to go out there than to listen to her mom complain about her ungrateful daughter all week.

On the farm, she could finally get her reading done. Just snuggle down on the couch and read all day with few interruptions. It seemed her mother wanted her there all weekend but didn't always want to talk to her or do anything special with her. Just having her only child present was enough for her mom most of the time, which left her with a lot of reading time.

But when it snowed or threatened to snow, Sara and Chester Kennedy would not come to get their daughter. She was stuck in town for the weekend.

A snowy weekend usually meant that she got to closet herself in her apartment and do what she loved to do most. But as much as she loved reading romance novels all weekend, she much preferred writing them, something she never did at her mom's house.

Grabbing a pop from the fridge, she left her nice apartment and went across the hall to her office. Sitting down, she swiped the mouse so the computer would come to life.

Looking around, she remembered when she moved in across the hall, there was a forty-year-old divorced guy who lived in the place before she took it over. Up until the time she had moved in, he had lived there alone. He had been there when she had been happy with Franky, and he had been there when Franky had outgrown her.

By April of that first year, when the snow was almost completely melted, Franky still wasn't coming home. Medical issues suddenly took her to the same town he was going to school in, and she was hospitalized for weeks. Even then, he still didn't have time to visit her. Just as she was being released from the hospital weeks later, he finally showed up, only to say that he had met someone else and that they were over.

Ruth came home, and with nothing else going on in her life, she just kept working for Frank. Franky graduated, married, and started a family. Ruth just worked for Frank. Should she have left? Maybe. But for years, she didn't think about it, just worked. Unable to move on.

Oddly, Frank never treated her any differently after the breakup. He just never talked about his son with her anymore. Over the years, the picture on his desk changed: Wedding, one baby, two babies, and then three. Frank never said a thing.

Still, the guy lived there until one day he was simply gone. She never asked where he went, and Frank never said if he knew. All that was left was the old couch and a few dishes that she threw out. After that, the apartment had stayed empty until she took it over.

It was only the day he told her he was retiring that he talked about Franky and what the younger man had done to her. That was the day he offered to sell her the building that she lived and worked in. The insurance business would be sold separately. Ruth immediately agreed since she hadn't spent a penny on rent since she'd moved in. She had been saving for something.

So, now she owned the entire building. Oddly, she didn't think Anderson Miles knew. Every month he had her mail the rent check to the owner, never letting on that it was her. And when something was broken, it was her job to call to get it repaired.

Once she had taken ownership of the building, she still had money in savings and started to look around town. Quickly and quietly, she had bought five other buildings downtown. Some had been for sale for years, including the one next door where Tess lives and the building across from them that Mia lived in, which now housed the only clinic in a forty-mile radius. Ruth was one of the biggest property owners in town if you exclude all those who have farmland.

She had learned to love the beginning of the month; the money would roll in. Most people who rented from her didn't know it was Ruth Kennedy that owned the building. When she had bought her first building, she had hired a rental managing company to do all the dirty work for her. Mia was one of the few renters that brought a check to her on the first of the month. Oddly, the town's biggest gossip had never told anyone else that Ruth owned the buildings; she just dropped it off and headed back to work. Sometimes they didn't even say a word to each other.

In the first year she had worked for Frank, she had realized that being Frank's secretary was kind of boring, especially during the early afternoon when he would nap in his office. That first summer, she started to write fun things to send to Franky to read, just to kill time. Most she was sure went unread by her lover, who wasn't into love notes. When he stopped coming home, she slowed down on the notes and started writing other things instead. It then evolved into the kind of books she was reading at the time.

The summer after Franky had dumped her, she had sold her first book. Since then, she wrote around eight books a year, sometimes more. Now she wrote under four pen names for different types of books, all from her drab, boring office.

Four years ago, when Anderson had bought the company and kept her on as his secretary, she thought she would have to stop writing at work. And she had, now only editing during working hours. He had never questioned what she did to fill her time, and she just had to be a bit more secretive about it.

Sometimes she felt guilty that she used her work time to write for personal gain. Then she felt guilty that he had to pay her rent for the building also. But so far, she had gotten everything done he had ever asked her to. He could probably get by without her, but he kept her on.

On top of that, she got to spend her days writing about people falling in love while watching Anderson just being handsome and sexy in his office. Guilty pleasures. For four years, no matter what her hero looked like on paper, in her head he always looked like Anderson.

Until recently, he had spent almost every weekend back in Grand Forks, where he came from and where he lived with his girlfriend. Can it be called 'living with' if he was only there on the weekends? The woman never even came to Landstad; he had always gone there. How they had kept that relationship going for so long, Ruth didn't know, but now it was over.

Now he was around on the weekends, though she usually wasn't. But today they were both at the café together, and he was all sexy in a brown sweater. His hair was even styled a little differently. She wondered if she was drooling when she had seen him there. Then Rafferty had wrecked it.

Rafferty. She cringed at Tess's suggestion that they were sexually attracted to each other. Even when they had been in high school and were only friends, there was never anything more than that. In fact, she had so few conversations with him that she wondered how they could live in the same small town. Now she knew that he was friends with Anderson, which was no fun.

CHAPTER 4

THAT MONDAY MORNING, Ruth was running late, which was very unusual for her. Usually, she was up early and just killing time until eight rolled around. But today she had overslept and had gotten out of bed closer to seven, but she hadn't wanted to get out of bed then either.

Even now she didn't know how many whiskeys she'd had the day before, but it was more than she could handle. The afternoon had been fun, and the three of them had turned to a few more because Mia had invited her cousin Amanda Nordskov, the same woman whose car had been stuck Friday night. Not that Ruth had cared, but it was just getting to be a lot of people for a small gathering. But instead of leaving like she usually did, she stayed.

Amanda had taken the time to thank her for helping dig her out of the snow and then explained the entire scene to the group, only she had made it seem far funnier than it had been. Apparently, Amanda had noticed Ruth hadn't been wearing a jacket that night, and Ruth still couldn't tell her exactly why. Nor did she mention the sexual tension between Amanda and Hue—that was something the entire group would find out...eventually.

Besides Amanda, Natalie Beckett from the library and a local girl

Hazel May had crashed also. They had come separately, and once they saw the other was there, both nearly bolted. Years before, there had been an accident involving them both when they were teenagers. Ruth did remember the accident, but she hadn't really known anyone who had been involved at the time. From what Mia had insinuated, the women were still affected by it and had not spoken to each other in years. Ruth had noticed they didn't say anything to one another in the café either.

At Mia's insistence, whiskey had been brought out, and everyone had a shot or two to take the edge off. Since nobody ended up leaving, it worked. Soon everyone was relaxed, even Ruth. After that, the group had chatted, mostly about the books they had read and wanted to read. Nothing was brought up about the town drama, which was a relief.

They all decided that the club would meet in two weeks again, and Ruth hoped everyone would come back. It was decided that they would each would read a different book and then compare and contrast. The next meeting would be at Ruth's since they all decided that they wanted to drink, and Mia really wasn't supposed to have drinks at her café even when it was closed.

Heading down the steps at five after eight, Ruth slipped into the office. At least being late had taken her mind off falling into a snow-bank over the weekend with her boss and all the embarrassment that entailed. Walking over to her desk, she slid into the seat and cursed. *Coffee.* Getting up again, she poured a cup for her boss. It was a tiny secretary move that she secretly enjoyed most days. Maybe it was to feed her addiction to his smell—he smelled so good.

She took the cup into his office, where he sat looking over some papers spread over his desk. "Morning, Anderson, here is your coffee." *Yup, there it was, the Anderson smell.*

At her words, he looked up with his brown eyes and smiled at her. "Thank you, Ruth. You're late."

Unable to not smile back at him, she said the first excuse that came to mind. "Weather."

Walking out of the office, she looked out the window at the sun glistening off the snow piles on the street outside. Maybe she should have paid more attention to what the actual weather was outside during her quick walk in. After sitting down at her desk, she slid her heels off and started getting her computer and phone ready for the week.

As usual, she could see him working at his desk from her own spot in the outer room. The office was good-sized, but she had moved her desk so she could see him before he'd even started there. When she had first done it, she was happy she could keep an eye on Frank and have her computer face the wall so that nobody could see what she was doing. When Anderson had started, all the furniture had stayed where it was. He seemed to not think anything of the setup, and she didn't mind one bit.

All morning, he sat in his office working on his computer, shuffling around loose papers, and calling people. Nobody called in, and nobody came in for her to deal with. So, Ruth spent the morning proofreading what she had written on Saturday evening.

Jessa and Link (formerly Jack) were well on their way to their happily ever after. All she had to do was rip them apart and put them back together. It sounded cruel, but how were they to know that they were meant to be without a little drama?

As lunchtime neared, she slipped her shoes back on, took off her reading glasses, and went into his office. "Do you want me to run and get lunch?"

He looked up at her and blinked in slight confusion. Running his hands through his hair, he said, "Yes, sure."

"Do you want your usual?" Ruth asked as always. It was a ham and cheese sandwich; he could eat one every day. And he almost did, but she asked because she didn't want him to think she knew him that well.

"No, let's get something different." His brown eyes were looking at her in confusion, like he had never seen her before. Or maybe like he had but couldn't remember where.

"Okay...what?" She tripped over her words. Was he talking about lunch or something else?

She stopped mid-turn to look back at him, but his eyes were on his paper suddenly.

"I don't know," he answered vaguely as he continued to look at the papers.

Something was up with him today. He was distracted, even she could tell. Usually, he was super organized and efficient, but today his papers were everywhere, and he had called Ned Keller twice for the same thing. The desks were close enough for her to have overheard.

"I can't get you what you don't know. You can go today. Maybe the special will be what you want," she huffed, walking out to her desk. She sat down in her chair, still facing him, and glared at him.

"Okay, I will go." Getting up, he grabbed his jacket and slid it on. "What do you want?"

"The special," she answered. It didn't really matter what the special was; she got it. After having gotten lunch at the same café for over ten years, she knew everything they made, and like a dutiful daughter, she ate the special like her mom was forcing her to.

A bonus was that the special was usually a large portion, and years ago, she had made lunch her biggest meal of the day. She usually ate a light supper since she didn't want to waste a lot of time cooking just for herself in the evening. That was just a waste of time she could use elsewhere.

Anderson slammed the door on the way out of the building, and she wondered what was bothering him so much. She could tell his mood was off. Maybe getting lunch would bring his mood back to normal.

CHAPTER 5

THE COLD AIR hit Anderson's face like a slap, which was exactly what he needed to get his mind off Ruth Kennedy. Instantly, he wanted to go back into the office and make her go get lunch. It was her job to get lunch, not his. Well, it actually wasn't her job; she just usually did it. Besides, if she would have just gone and gotten the food, he would have eaten it happily.

But when she had walked in and asked what he wanted, he lost it. The light from the window was behind her, making her glow like never before, and suddenly he saw the woman in the snowbank, and he wanted to touch her again.

Suddenly, the same old thing wasn't good enough. He wanted different. He wanted the weekend Ruth, not the Ruth who worked for him, but there was no way he could actually say that.

All morning, he had watched her typing at her desk. What she could possibly spend the entire morning on was beyond him, but if it kept the office running smoothly, he didn't ask. They were a well-run team after all these years.

When she had been late, he had actually wondered if she had quit without telling him. Would she have quit because he was friends with Rafferty? Because of their run-in during the blizzard? Why else? Then she had breezed in without her coat on, and he was instantly mad. She was late and didn't even apologize, just blamed it on the weather. The roads were perfect this morning, and the sun was even shining. It was a beautiful day.

Ruth looked the exact same as she did every other Monday morning, except today he looked beyond her prim and proper attire and saw the wispy white hairs that were too short for the bun floating around her head. When she had sat down and kicked off her shoes, he noticed that she pulled her bare feet onto the chair under her butt. And she had slid those ugly black reading glasses on and stared at the screen in front of her. All business, with a touch of adorable that he had never noticed before.

At one point, he looked up, and she was chewing on a pencil as she stared at the screen. She was blushing scarlet from her hairline all the way to where her first two buttons on her blouse were open. And most likely further down. All he could do was picture it.

So, in reality, he had spent the morning thinking of his personal assistant naked. He had never even noticed her before, and then suddenly, he couldn't get the thought out of his head. Maybe it was Rafferty saying she used to do what teenagers do that brought up the images. But in his imagination, she was not a teenager; she was a very put-together professional with a hidden wild streak.

Warmth enveloped him as he entered the café and walked up to the counter, leaving his coat on since he was not staying. Mia was walking by but instead stopped in front of him, laughing. Over the years, he had struck up a sort of friendship with the woman, though they were not close.

"Anderson, did Angel call in sick? I knew she drank too much yesterday, but I didn't think it was that much," Mia continued to laugh as she started writing down the order, not even asking what she wanted.

"No, Ruth is there. Looks just fine, too. She was a little late but mostly on time," Anderson said to the waitress. Why was he explaining it to her?

"Ruth is a lightweight, and I know she had four shots, maybe more." Mia tapped her pen on her order pad. "The usuals, then?"

"Yeah," he replied, not thinking about the fact that he wanted something new. His mind was on whether or not Ruth was hungover. She didn't seem like it, but he didn't know what her hungover would be like. She seemed the same as always; it was him who was different. He wondered for a moment if he was hungover himself.

Resting his head in his hands as he waited for the food to be made, he wondered if he had changed the way he was looking at Ruth because he was suddenly single. Not that he and Daphne's relationship had been all that great for the past few years, but it had been enough for him. Now that it was over, he realized that in the past month, he hadn't missed her once. So maybe it had been time for it to end.

Within a few minutes, Mia had brought the lunches in white Styrofoam containers and placed them in front of him. "Wake up, Anderson. Did you drink too much yesterday, too?"

"No, not a drop yesterday, but Friday night was a doozy," he admitted, pulling out money to cover the bill.

"I hope you're not hanging with Rafferty now. He is not good company," Mia said as she got his change from the register.

"He's a nice enough guy. Do you know why he and Ruth do not get along?" Anderson asked since Mia was the pulse of the community. If she didn't know, nobody did.

"You will have to ask one of them. Neither has ever said, and I have never heard," Mia explained, which meant something since Mia always knew everything in this town.

"He said that he likes her, but she does not like him," Anderson informed her.

"Could be more his dad. She really does not get on with him. In fact, I have seen her walk out of rooms he was in on more than one occasion. Something to look into if you are interested enough to want to know," Mia said as she was called away by a customer.

Grabbing the white boxes, he headed back out into the cold and wondered what Howard Brooks could have done to Ruth. He didn't actually know the other insurance agent in town because he had not had much opportunity to talk to Rafferty's father. Howard didn't do a lot of work that Anderson could tell. Rafferty was carrying the load at the building down the street.

He walked in with the boxed lunches, pushing the door open to the office with his back. He set the warm one on her desk in front of her and took his cold one into the office. Sitting down, he heard Ruth laugh out loud, a sound he had rarely heard from her. It was a pleasant sound in the quiet rooms. Turning in her direction, she slid her reading glasses up on her head as she asked, "Did you tell Mia I was still drunk?"

"No. She thought you had called in sick. I told her you were a little late but not sick," Anderson defended himself, wondering where she had gotten the information about their conversation.

"She wrote in my box that I must be drunk still to let you get lunch, but she added that you are drunk too." She turned the styrofoam box her lunch was in so he could see the inside cover. He couldn't see any writing since they were ten feet apart.

"Funny," he said back to her, not remembering anything ever written in their boxes before.

"Are you drunk, Anderson?" She took her glasses off her head and put the earpiece in her mouth as she looked at him with those ice-blue eyes.

"Are you drunk, Angel?" He watched her, trying to not look at her mouth, and failing.

Instantly, the smile vanished from her that mouth. Now he had done it; he shouldn't have called her Angel. He could tell she wasn't happy with it.

"No, I am not. Even my headache has subsided now." She put her glasses on the desk with more concentration than was needed. "Please don't call me Angel. It's a weird nickname that only a few people still call me. Most people don't remember it."

"Just Mia and Rafferty?" he asked. Why was he pushing? Why was he jealous that Rafferty had a nickname for her?

"Mostly just people who graduated around me. And my mother; I don't think she even remembers my real name. She's called me that since I was born." There was no humor in her words.

"Ruth it is then," Anderson said and opened his container. Nothing was written in it, which was a little disappointing.

"Do you have a weird nickname that I can call you if you ever slip up?" she asked as she started to eat. Hers was meatloaf today. He could smell it from where he sat. It smelled good.

"Andy is about it, though that's not weird. It's just my name," he said, taking out his sandwich. He had wanted a change, but it looked the same as always, perfect.

"A change, Andy?" She noticed he had just gotten the same thing he always ordered and laughed, "Andy makes it sound like you are a little kid."

"But not weird." He smiled at her reaction to the name almost everyone back home called him. It was only here in Landstad that everyone called him Anderson, and probably because his personal assistant did. In the beginning, he thought about correcting people but didn't think he would be there that long, so he didn't bother.

"I will stick with Anderson unless you are very naughty, then I will go with Anderson Miles. What's your middle name?" Ruth went back to eating her lunch.

The images flashing through his mind at her saying 'naughty' made him swallow hard. Those images were definitely not for in the office. And suddenly he was back to picturing her naked.

"Everett," was all he could say as he turned his chair away from her view. She didn't need to see how her words had affected him. Or what effect she was having on him today, period.

"That is a nice one."

He tried to get his mind under control. "What's yours?"

"My what?" she asked as if she hadn't been a part of the conversation.

"Your middle name?"

"Oh, yeah. Ruth." She waved her fork in the air at the answer.

"So, Ruth Ruth?" he smirked.

"Oh, sorry, Mary Ruth. All good Catholics name their kids Mary.

Mary Ruth Johnson Kennedy." She closed her empty container and threw it in the garbage beside her desk. Same as every day.

"Two last names? Divorced?" He had never heard that she had married, but then again, he knew very little about her up until yesterday.

"No, never married. My mom had me add her husband's name when she got married. I was fourteen and didn't care. Now I think I would have skipped that and just stuck with Johnson. Too late now." She shrugged and turned away from him to look at her computer.

After finishing his sandwich, he threw away his box and said, "Thank you for the fun conversation over lunch, Ruth." He hated that it was over already.

"Anytime, Anderson. I am usually right here." But she didn't look at him as she said it, just at her computer. Then without looking away from the screen, she blindly grabbed for her glasses until she found them and put them on without looking away from the screen. Her other hand was typing at the same time.

Turning back to his work, he couldn't concentrate on the paper in front of him. Just like this morning, his mind was on the woman in the front of the office staring at her computer screen. And she was naked in those images, except those glasses had now become a focal point of the scene.

CHAPTER 6

"ANOTHER WEEK OF BELOW-ZERO WEATHER. So, no nice weather until at least after February 1st." Ruth looked up from the weather report app on her cellphone. Anderson was sitting at his desk with his feet up. This was their usual quiet time, and during these quiet weeks, she wondered when he would notice that she didn't do much around there. Because there was nothing to do.

"Is your mom coming to get you today?" he asked. It was Friday, and at five, her mother would be waiting outside the door in her old Buick to whisk her away to the farm. It was something that had happened nearly every Friday.

"Too cold this weekend. Mom does not like going out when it is too cold, and Chester does whatever my mom says," she said, putting her phone down and sliding her glasses off so she could see him clearly. Sometimes she left them on when she talked to him so that she didn't see his handsome face across the room. It was very distracting sometimes.

It had been close to a month since book club had started, and this weekend was the third meet-up. They were again meeting at Ruth's place because of their need and want to drink. It also made sure that the entire town didn't know about it and want to join in—six members were enough, a number Ruth had gotten used to faster than she had expected to.

Since the first meeting, the book club had changed. They were still reading books, but each of them was reading a different book, so their discussion was more about the murders and not the books themselves. But Natalie had expressed an interest in making their conversations into a podcast, like a radio show that could be found on the internet. This week was going to be the first one they would record. Ruth was a bit nervous about the whole thing, but the others seemed to be excited about it, or at least pretended to. She was eighty percent sure only Natalie was actually excited about the recording part.

In that time at the office, Anderson had started talking to her more than ever before. No longer was it just mundane conversations about the weather or town happenings or work. Now they were talking about more personal things. The weather still came up a lot, but it was winter in North Dakota, so it was always on everyone's mind.

With the change, she was sometimes unable to edit during the afternoon because they were talking, and it was cutting into her work time. But learning more about Anderson was worth the wasted work time. Work would always be there; Anderson, not so much.

"Any big plans for the weekend then?" Anderson asked as he now did on Fridays.

"No, just book club on Sunday afternoon." She was looking through the papers on her desk.

"What book this week?" He had wormed some of the names out of her of who was in book club. *Okay, he knows them all!* He was very good at getting information from her.

"*Fifty Shades of Gray,*" she smirked. He knew the book; everyone knew the book. The group had agreed to tell everyone that was the book—it kept the older generation from wanting in if they ever found out about it. It was actually about the *Son of Sam,* but she wasn't telling him that. Or that her book had been interesting but graphic in a different way than the book she had told him.

"Learn anything new?" He grinned at her.

"Nothing I didn't already know." She was proud of herself for not blushing. At thirty, she hated that she blushed so easily. It was her cross to bear for having such pale skin. She also never tanned, just burned to a crisp.

The door to the outside opened, letting in a cold chill and stopping their conversation. Ruth gathered the sweater off her chair and pulled it over her shoulders. Looking up at the visitor, she lost her smile. "Anderson, your friend is here."

Anderson got to his feet and came out to her office area. "Rafferty, what can I do for you today? Come into my office; my personal assistant has some issues with you."

Rafferty looked over at Ruth. "I actually want to talk with her for a minute."

"I have nothing to say to you, Brooks." Ruth was again shuffling through the papers on her desk, though she had no idea what she was even looking for anymore. Her only thoughts were what he could possibly want from her.

"I need you to talk to Mia for me. Talk me up." He grabbed a visitor chair and pulled it to the front of her desk and plopped down in it, not caring that Anderson was listening still.

"No, I don't want any of my friends talking to you. They deserve better." She didn't look up at him.

"You owe me, Angel," he mumbled quietly. She knew he was staring at her.

She stood up and looked down at him with anger. "And this is what you want? Mia? What happens when you need a liver?" Her voice was quiet, but she knew Anderson could hear anyway.

"I hear yours is getting quite the workout at book club, so it might not be in the best shape." He stared her in the eyes as he got to his feet, the smile gone.

"Not nearly as much as yours always has," she countered. He was a social drinker, and he was always socializing. Or more accurately, he was a player and spent most of his off time at the bar.

"Could you just talk to her?" he asked, nicer now, maybe a little whiny.

"No. If she wants to talk to you, she will. She knows you as well as

I do." She picked up the pile of papers because she had nothing else to actually do to look busy.

It wasn't like Mia would listen to her; they were new friends, nothing more. And if she even thought that Mia would want to date Rafferty, she didn't need Ruth's assistance in that. They worked not a block apart every day. Rafferty spent more time in the cafe than Ruth herself did.

"Come on, Angel," he pleaded, adding again in case she forgot. "You owe me."

"No, Mia is her own person and doesn't listen to me. And if she did, I would tell her to stay as far from you as possible. So I wouldn't even ask," she whispered and sat down, then turned her back to him. Though she had nothing to do behind her desk, she just stared at the wall.

Once she heard him walk into Anderson's office, she turned back to her computer and started doing actual work. Editing. Time to get back to that. But the conversation in Anderson's office drew her attention and distracted her.

"Dad just sold the building our office is in. Someone offered him way more than it was worth, and he took it," Rafferty was saying. From the side position, she could see him sitting in one of the chairs across from Anderson. He didn't look as relaxed as usual.

"So now you have rent. I rent this place. It's not bad, and you don't have to worry about taxes and upkeep. When something breaks, you just call the management company, and it gets fixed." Anderson tried to make it sound like a good thing, which it was. Maintenance was expensive on an old building.

"No, they want us out. They doubled the average rent price in the area. Dad is retiring, but I need the office. I don't want to leave town, but I might have to," Rafferty said.

"Maybe somewhere else in town?" Anderson asked.

"No luck. They own almost all the open rental space in town." Rafferty leaned back and rubbed his eyes hard.

"I rent from M Johnson Inc., and I haven't had any issues." Anderson was leaning towards his friend.

Ruth looked in at the men who were talking about her without even knowing it. Howard Brooks had lied to his son. The building was up for sale and at below market value. Ruth had snapped it up the first day it was on the market. She had plans. They mostly involved forcing Rafferty and his father from town. It was a perfect plan.

"That's who bought the building. We've been there since before I was even born, and now we are going to have to move," Rafferty explained. She could hear the pain in his voice. It kind of made her giddy.

"Well, if your dad retired, maybe you'd want to join me over here," Anderson suggested, and Ruth could tell he was smiling. She knew his smiles from any angle.

Ruth jumped up from her desk and rushed into Anderson's office; things had taken a bad turn. "No way is he working here. I will be out that door if he comes in it. I will not spend my days working with him."

"Ruth, it was just an idea," Anderson stated, his eyes showing shock at her reaction.

"We could be co-workers, Angel. It would be fun. You, me, and Andy, a trio of insurance fun." Rafferty grinned at her. He knew she would hate the idea.

"I will quit. In fact, why don't you just think about how my quitting would affect you because I am leaving right now. Have a good weekend!" she yelled through the door at them as she turned off her computer without saving anything, which in itself said how mad she was. Then she stormed out the door.

Outside, she didn't even feel the cold on the short walk. Stomping up the stairs to her apartment, she kicked off her shoes in the hallway and realized she'd forgotten her coat. It was twenty below zero, and she had forgotten her coat. Then again, if she needed it by Monday, she had a key to the office. Perks of owning the building.

After pulling her hair from its bun, she stripped off her clothes and yanked on a pair of leggings and a sweatshirt. Slipping on comfortable socks and slippers, she sat down on the couch and turned on the TV in the corner. She rarely watched it, but she was in no mood to write anything today. Anger was still coursing through her.

Rafferty Brooks was going to kick her out of a job. Rafferty Brooks gets everything, even though she had been working for years to take everything from him. Last month she had purchased the building he worked in to force them out, and now he was just going to take her job from her. How was it that he always came out ahead in a war that he didn't even know she was waging?

It wasn't even that she loved the job that much; she just liked to see people every now and then. In reality, she made more money from her rental properties than working for Anderson and more money from writing than working for Anderson and her rental properties combined. But she worked for Anderson so that she could see him five days a week.

Rafferty was going to ruin everything.

CHAPTER 7

ANDERSON WATCHED Ruth head out the door into the sub-zero weather without a coat on and walk past the front window in just a blue blouse that was barely enough for the chilly office. In fact, she usually slipped on a sweater during the cooler days. Jumping from his chair, he grabbed her coat and followed her to give her the much-needed piece of clothing. But when he pushed out the door and looked down the street, she was gone. Completely disappeared, just like the night of the blizzard. Heading out, he walked down the street, looking in cars to see if she was waiting for hers to warm up. He didn't find her, nor were there any cars driving down the street.

Finally, the cold sent him back to the office to get his coat to keep looking for her. His usually unemotional personal assistant had blown her top at him because of Rafferty. He knew he should have talked to her before he said what he did to Rafferty, but the man was his friend, and he was falling on hard times.

"Find her?" Rafferty asked with a little smirk. The man didn't seem to care for Ruth's safety and health. He just seemed to like to antagonize her.

"No, I think she is in the parking lot down the street," he said, sliding on his jacket as quickly as he could. "She must be freezing."

"Why would she be down there?" Rafferty asked as he too was slipping on his jacket to help.

"I didn't see her on the street. I am pissed I don't even know what she drives," Anderson admitted. To his credit, he had never seen her driving or walking to her car. She usually got to work after him and left before him, but now he realized they should talk about where she parks. Just basic safety things like that.

"Probably still the 1970 Dodge Charger with the big engine. It is most likely in Chester's garage for the winter," Rafferty replied, pulling his jacket off.

Looking over at his friend, he asked, "Green?"

"Yup." Rafferty sat down in one of the waiting room chairs. It seemed he was no longer going to help look for her.

"I have seen that in the summer. What does she drive in the winter?" Anderson wanted to know, needed to know. That car was not a daily driver. He may not know a lot about cars, but he knew that.

The car was usually sitting outside the office door when it was in town. For a month or two in the summer, it sat there, right by the window. Then it was gone, not to be seen for another year.

"Nothing. She doesn't go far in the winter, and Chester or Sara come and get her on the weekends." Rafferty moved the visitor chair back to where it had been before he'd come into the office.

"How far does she walk to work then? She needs her coat," Anderson said, holding it up for him to see as if he didn't know what the conversation was about.

"She is already home, don't worry about it." Rafferty sat down in the chair and dropped his arms over the chairs on either side of him.

"How close does she live, Rafferty?" Anderson demanded. Why did his friend know where she lived, but he, her boss, did not?

"Very." Rafferty could barely contain his smirk. In fact, he didn't. "You have no idea where she lives? Really?" He raised an eyebrow in question.

"Where does she live?" Anderson demanded, hanging the coat back on the hook.

Rafferty's answer was to point to the ceiling. Anderson looked up as if she was going to be floating above his head.

"She has lived upstairs forever. I can't believe you have never known. You never noticed?" Rafferty couldn't stop smiling.

"Forever?" he asked, sliding his jacket off. With sudden realization, he knew where she had vanished to the night of the blizzard across the street. Turning, he actually looked at the spot, though the snow pile had long ago been moved.

Then a lot of their conversations ran through his mind, such as her always blaming being late because of the weather, that he never saw her car, and that she was always walking around town when he saw her. Always walking. But if she lived here, then she didn't have far to go to get anywhere.

"I think she moved in while she and Franky were still engaged. Frank always let her live up there when he owned the building. I heard she was rent-free the entire time. Guilt over what his kid did." Rafferty followed him back to his office, away from Ruth's desk and the window so he couldn't look out without seeing her in that snowbank.

"You think?" Anderson asked, wanting to know more about Ruth. He suddenly wanted to know everything about her.

"I don't know exactly. We were no longer all that close, and I went to college. But it is a small town; you hear things over the years."

No wonder her mother picked her up every week from work—she was also at home. He wondered why she never went home for lunch since it was right there. Instead, they ordered in all the time. Lately, they had been talking more over lunch than ever before. Nothing serious, just little things. He liked to see if he could make her laugh. Most days he was successful.

"You suddenly seem way too into Angel, Anderson. Are you interested in her?" Rafferty asked, humor gone from his demeanor.

"No, I am not," he said a little too quickly. He wasn't admitting anything to Rafferty that he wasn't ready to admit to himself.

"Go for it if you want to, but her mother will kill you. She doesn't let much happen to Ruth. She's a bit overprotective. Always has been," Rafferty informed him seriously.

Anderson had never seen the woman beyond her head in a late model Buick. She never came in to get Ruth. Ruth had to go out to her. Not that he was interested in Ruth, so it didn't matter.

"Let's go get some drinks," Anderson said, standing up. Rafferty followed him, and they grabbed their coats and headed out into the cold dark street only lit by streetlights. It was North Dakota in January, so it was dark by five. While walking across the street, Anderson couldn't help but look up and the windows above the insurance office. There was a soft glow behind the curtains in the windows. He shook his head, pretending he didn't care that she lived there.

CHAPTER 8

AFTER A FEW HOURS of mindlessly watching TV, Ruth was almost back to her old unflustered self. During the movie, she had come up with a plan to get Rafferty to stay away from her and her job. It involved backing off on the rent at his office for a while. Maybe by then, Anderson would have forgotten about asking Rafferty to work there. Or better yet, he'd realize he would rather have Ruth than Rafferty working with him.

Smiling, she turned off the TV and grabbed a pop from the fridge, then headed to her office. Now she could work. As she walked across the hallway, she stopped to straighten the shoes lined up by the door. *No need for disorder*, she thought to herself. Opening the door, she was met by the whirling of the equipment. Comforting whirling.

Sitting at her desk, she set her phone down and noticed she had a text from Mia.

> **Mia:** Go out with me tonight. I need a drink.
> **Mia:** Please!!!!!
> **Ruth:** No, already settled for the night.
> **Mia:** Put on a bra and have one with me.

Smiling, she shut the computer back down. If any day was a day to go out for a drink, today was the day.

Ruth: I think a drink would be good after today.

Walking back to her apartment, she twisted her hair into a loose bun on her head and put on jeans and a blue sweater. Sliding on her shoes, she walked down to the bottom of the stairs and, without a jacket, she ran across the street. No need to grab the thing since Mia's was across the street and the bar was just a block down. And besides, her coat was still locked in the office.

Once she opened the door to the stairway up to Mia's place, she yelled up the steps, "I am here!"

She heard a door open, then footsteps on the floor above. Mia's building had two apartments, but only one was occupied right now. The other was one of her only vacancies.

Mia leaned over the side of the railing of the stairways and said, "Don't let my landlord hear you yelling in the hallway. We have rules against that sort of thing."

Ruth laughed at her joke. Mia was one of few people who knew she owned this building or any other for that matter. Mia always walked her check over to her on the first of the month. Lately, it had turned into a fun ritual and not just a chore to get over with. Mia had grown on her in the last few weeks, and she understood why Mia was loved by so many people.

Mia looked down at her in question. "Are you bringing a coat?"

"No, I left it at work, and the bar is right there." She shrugged.

"It's cold," Mia said but took off her coat.

"We will be outside for two minutes."

"We will run then." Mia bounded down the stairs without her coat on.

So, they did, running the block and a half to the only bar in town, The Landing. Both pushed into the building, laughing as they almost fell over each other in their rush to get inside. Mia hadn't worn a sweater, so she must have been colder than Ruth was. Getting to their feet, Mia called out to the bartender. "Paul, two whiskeys to warm us up."

"No whiskey for me, just something mixed, Paul." Ruth walked over to a table that Mia had pointed to. Having not spent much time in the bar, Ruth looked around as she sat down. It had not actually changed since she had come in here to eat with her mom before she married Chester; back then, her mom loved nothing more than spending her evenings in this very bar. Things changed when she had gotten married. Now she pretends that she had never even been in the bar, much less been a regular.

Mia sat down across from her and said, "I am going to text Tess. She should come out too."

True to her word, Mia started texting their friend. When the drinks showed up, it wasn't the bartender who delivered them but Rafferty Brooks. As he set them down, he said, "And I thought you were against favors, Angel."

"Rafferty, just leave them alone. Ruth is going to throw her drink at you." Anderson cut in, pulling the other man away. Anderson was not wrong. She had been eyeing up the drink as to how far she could throw it.

Within minutes, Tess Thorn walked into the room, tearing Ruth's focus away from the men at the bar. The older woman walked in, making Ruth feel all rushed and sloppy. Tess was wearing a tight leather jacket, skin-tight tailored jeans, and boots with a four-inch heel.

Mia slammed her drink down and yelled, "Dress down, lady! You are making us all look bad. This is Landstad!"

Ruth just laughed at her friend's words. They were so true. Tess was always so well put together, and Ruth had yet to see her dressed down. Ruth was pretty sure the woman had no comfy clothes; she was just always like this.

Tess stopped at the bar and ordered a glass of wine before she came over to them and slid in next to Mia. "Ladies."

"Should we text Mandy?" Tess looked around the bar.

"No, she's in Grand Forks," Mia stated. Since they were cousins and neighbors, Mia knew about Mandy's movements, even beyond the entire town gossip thing.

"Should we call Natalie and Hazel?" Mia scooted over. The two of them were in their early twenties, which made Ruth feel old sometimes when they made references to things she had no clue about.

"No, Hazel has the baby, and Natalie should be with her fiancé today." Ruth knew both of the women had a ton of responsibility. Hazel had a young son, and Natalie was getting married the next summer.

"Everyone had a bad day?" Tess asked the group.

"You got that right." Ruth glared again at Rafferty, wishing Anderson would move so that she didn't have to glare angrily at him too. His only crime was being friends with the enemy. Why must he be friends with the enemy?

Turning back to the girls, she saw that they were both staring at her. "What? Rafferty Brooks killed my day."

"He always seemed harmless to me." Tess sipped her wine and glanced over at the two men at the bar with amusement.

"Has he turned his smooth moves on you? He likes to bang anything in a skirt." Mia downed her shot of whiskey, then slammed her hand to her mouth. "No offense, Tess. Your skirts are always nice. And yours too, Ruth."

Tess just laughed at the now purple-haired woman beside her. "No, Mia, I have not had the attention of Mr. Brooks. I think I am a little too old for him, anyway." Tess looked into her glass.

"Too old? That has never been an issue with that one." Mia waved to the bartender for another drink.

"Then I think I am going to have hurt feelings since he has yet to pursue me." Tess looked over the man in question again.

"Don't waste your time with him," Ruth said. "Anyway, he has a thing for Mia right now."

Mia's eyes flew to the man in question. "He can keep his thing to himself."

"So, there is a hot man who has a job and great hair, and you want nothing to do with him, Mia. Why?" Tess asked the waitress.

"Because he is Rafferty. And besides, the minute I get enough money together, I am out of this town. I am a big-city girl trapped in this dinky town, always have been. Rafferty would only mess that up. And he is a player," Mia pointed out. Though as far as Ruth had heard lately, he hadn't dated anyone in months.

"I would play with that if he was looking at me like he is looking at you." Tess laughed at Mia, who had started to shake her head in denial.

Paul brought over drinks for the table and indicated that they had been paid for by the guys. Once he left, Mia leaned into the table and whispered, "I tapped that once. Not going back."

"Who? Paul?" Ruth asked in shock. The bartender was almost two decades older than they were. Even though the women had known each other most of their entire lives, Ruth thought she would have heard about that one.

"No, Rafferty. Long time ago, ancient history now. But still a history not worth repeating." Mia downed her new glass of whiskey.

Ruth had moved on to her new drink and liked whatever it was that Paul had made. Deciding Rafferty was not going to ruin her night, she turned to Tess and asked, "So how old are you, anyway?"

Tess turned back to her and looked over at her. "How old are you, Ruth?"

Mia jumped in. "She turns the big thirty-one pretty soon, sometime in late winter if I remember right. Mine is in the fall, and I will be twenty-nine. I need to be out of this town by thirty."

Tess looked over at the woman. "I will never get over how much you know about people. Do you know the name, age, and address of everyone in this bar?"

Mia looked around her at the twenty or so people in the bar. Looking back at Tess, she answered, "All but you. I'm sorry, I am a people person. I cannot change that for you."

"That's what makes me say you can never leave this town. It will fall apart without you." Tess waved at the bartender again.

"I know, the café would be sad without Mia yelling at someone for something. Never going to be the same." Ruth agreed with Tess.

Anderson walked up to the table with the drinks this time. Ruth noticed he had taken his jacket and tie off and was just in his white button-down shirt and had opened the first few buttons. God, he looked good relaxed. Sadly, he looked good anytime. And maybe even better after she'd had a few drinks.

After setting the glasses on the table, he handed them out and said, "Peace offering from Rafferty and me. Our hope is to get back into your good graces, ladies."

Tess looked him up and down. "It will take more than a few drinks to put yourselves right with these ladies. More drinks and one of those little cardboard pizzas might help."

Anderson laughed, saluted her, and went back to the bar. "Coming right up."

Watching him walk away, she decided that her limit might be two. Then she started drinking the new one that Anderson had brought over. Turning back to the girls, she saw that they were both staring right at her. "What?"

"You have the hots for your boss," Mia replied in a whisper that wasn't exactly the quiet whisper of a sober woman.

"I do not."

"Oh, she does. He's a fine one, too. Should I head out and leave you guys to them?" Tess asked.

"No!" both women said at the same time, and all three broke out laughing.

The conversation turned away from her and who she had the hots for. And what did it matter if she did have the hots for her boss? He didn't even notice her. For four nice years, she had been able to just look at him for forty hours a week. It was never going to go anywhere; they were completely different. One day, he would be gone. He was not staying here forever, unlike her.

"Did you hear that Howard Brooks sold the insurance office?" Mia pulled Ruth's attention back to the conversation.

"Not the insurance part, just the building," Ruth answered. Mia's eyes swung to Ruth, who just smiled at her and took a sip of her drink. Now Mia knew who the buyer was.

"I heard that they might be evicted; rent is going to be too high."

Mia's eyes didn't leave Ruth's face. She knew where the answers to her questions would have to come from: Ruth.

"That's what I heard also," Ruth confirmed but didn't go into it any more than that.

"Someone must really hate Rafferty to do that." Mia's eyes slid to the man in question at the bar.

"Rafferty is just an annoyance. Somebody really hates his father," Ruth stated. Rafferty had done nearly nothing to her, except he was his father's child. Guilty by association.

The man in question walked over to the table with another round of drinks. Nobody thanked him as he set them down, but he was all smiles anyway. He then walked away without saying anything, and the ladies watched him go.

"Doesn't seem so bad to me," Tess commented, not catching the underlying conversation happening at the table.

"Wait till he opens his mouth." Ruth took a sip of her drink.

"I can't drink these. I am already buzzed," Mia said from the back of the booth.

Ruth turned to Mia, who was sitting behind two glasses of whiskey, and two empty ones were piled in front of her. Tess handed her a full glass of wine and took the two glasses and downed them before anyone could say anything. Smiling, she added the empties to Mia's pile.

"I am never having a drinking contest with you," Mia said in amazement.

"Drink your wine, you lightweight." Tess patted her back.

"I could have drunk them; I just shouldn't. I have to walk home after this. You know the rules about drinking and walking. Friends don't let friends walk home drunk." Mia laughed at herself.

Tess looked at her and got up, heading to the bar. She talked to Paul for a moment and then spent a few minutes talking to a man who was sitting at the bar that Ruth didn't know by name, but knew he was from town. Coming back, she carried four whiskeys. Setting them on the table, she slid into the booth again. "Sorry, I drank your whiskeys, Mia. I got you extra as a peace offering."

Mia's eyes were as big as saucers looking at the four full glasses. Taking one, she drank almost all of it before setting it down. "Bluff called, Tess. I am a lightweight."

Tess and Ruth laughed at Mia's defeat. Ruth watched as Tess took the glasses from in front of Mia and quickly drank the three full ones and then finished off the one Mia hadn't finished, then added the empty glasses to the pile in front of Mia. Ruth realized that the woman across from her had now consumed more alcohol than Mia and her combined but seemed completely sober as she started sipping her wine again.

Just as the pizza showed up, Tess said that she should head out. That left Mia and Ruth alone with the pizza. They ate and talked about people that they knew and what had happened to them over the years. It was actually a lot of fun to gossip with Mia, who knew everyone and everything in the town.

Since their drinks stopped going down so fast, the guys had stopped bringing them more. Now they were just nursing the last of what had been brought before the pizza came. Ruth barely noticed Anderson and Rafferty at the bar anymore. In the last hour, the building had filled up. The noise level rose, and Ruth was not used to being anywhere with this many people. She was about ready to leave.

As they talked, she noticed that Anderson was talking to Heather Reed, who was recently divorced. The woman was definitely into Anderson, and he seemed to be interested in her. It was starting to bother Ruth to watch. Sure, he had lived with someone for years, but she never had that rubbed in her face. Not like this.

A younger woman had stopped and talked to Mia and was asking Mia to join her group in the back of the bar. Ruth glanced at the table of around seven women who were singing and dancing and having a good time. Mia was saying that she was okay with Ruth and that they should have a good time without her.

But Ruth could tell that Mia really wanted to go and spend time with her real friends. Most likely, she had just called Ruth to come out when nobody else answered. Mia hadn't really wanted to spend time with boring Ruth Kennedy, now that her real friends were here. It was time to go.

"You go with your friends, Mia. I should go home anyway," Ruth mumbled as she got up quickly. Too quickly because her head started spinning, and she had to sit down again, hard. She bumped the table, making some of the glasses fall over, which then sent alcohol and ice running over the table.

Before she could process what had happened, Rafferty was in front of her. "Are you okay, Angel? You know you shouldn't drink like that."

"I am fine. Get away from me, Rafferty." She pushed him away from her. Getting to her feet, she was less dizzy this time and was able to walk away. Pushing through the front door, the freezing cold hit her hard, taking her breath away. At the same time, it cooled down her utter embarrassment of almost passing out.

Instead of running back to her apartment, she walked slowly and enjoyed the bite of the cold on her bare skin. Oddly, she knew that she could get frost bite at these temperatures, but she didn't care. Maybe she was drunker than she thought.

"Ruth, wait!" Anderson called to her.

Glancing behind her, she winced as she watched him hurrying to catch up with her. He had his bulky winter jacket on and was carrying his suit jacket. "I'm fine, Anderson. You can go back to the bar."

"I am going to make sure you get home." He slowed as he caught up with her.

"You don't need to do that. I can get there myself," she assured him.

"Where is your car?" He was looking around the street.

"It's over there. I can get there myself. Good night, Anderson." She loved that he didn't know she lived above the office. It was a fun secret.

"Mary Ruth Kennedy, you are lying to me. Right to my face in the middle of Main Street in the freezing cold." He took her hand to walk across the street.

"Damn it," she whispered. He knew. Rafferty had such a big mouth.

He stopped at her door. "Get inside."

Pushing her into the little landing at the bottom of the stairs, she stopped. The spot that they were standing was small, tall but tight. It held on to the cold that the thin glass door didn't keep out. They were standing so close that his coat was brushing up to her sweater. Looking into his dark brown eyes, she saw the desire for her in them. But she knew it was the alcohol and not anything real.

"Ask me up, Ruth." His eyes were on hers, and his voice was a husky whisper.

"For drinks? I have had enough," she whispered, wishing he would touch her.

"No drinks." He ran a hand lightly over her hair.

"Sex?" she whispered the word that was making the cold room sizzle around them, despite the fact that she could see her breath this close to the outside door.

"Yes." His mouth lowered towards hers slowly.

She pushed at his chest before he could kiss her. "I am not going to be your drunk hookup, Anderson. Go back to Heather Reed for that." Spinning, she ran up the stairs away from him. Would he follow? Stopping and leaning against the hallway wall as she kicked off her shoes, she didn't hear him on the steps. Holding her breath, she tried not to breathe too loudly until she heard the outside door open as he left.

Entering her apartment, she wondered if that had actually happened. Was she so drunk she dreamed it? Then she wondered why she had stopped it if it was real. Yes, she was totally willing to be his drunk hookup. When had she turned into a prude? Maybe it had happened in the last dozen years since she actually had hooked up with someone.

After changing back into her comfortable clothes, she sat down on the couch with a glass of cold water, turning on the TV to take her mind off the end of the great evening. It had been so much fun to get together with friends and have a laugh about life. It was also fun to see Anderson out of the office. It was nice to be a part of a world she had never been included in, but then it had come crashing down around her, and she was reminded that she didn't belong there with them.

Ruth was the outsider who grew up in this town. Born there,

raised there, and had never left. But being included had never been an option for her. She had been raised by her single, religious mother with no father in the picture. In school, she had been shy and quiet, unable to connect easily with kids who she had been in school with. During her last years of high school, she had a small group of friends, but they had mostly been Franky's. Rafferty was the only one in that group that was even still around.

After the break-up, she had removed herself from society for a few years, unable to cope with the whispers and stares. Yet she was unable to move away either; her mother needed her close. Now she was thirty and had nothing to show for it. Few friends, little family. Her large property holdings and writing didn't keep her warm at night.

Maybe she should look at moving to a larger town. She could sell her properties and move on with her life. Once she had stayed in hopes that Franky would come back for her, but now she stayed because she had no ambition to go anywhere else. Maybe getting fired would be the best thing for her, forcing her out of her comfortable hiding place.

CHAPTER 9

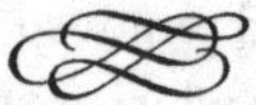

ANDERSON ANGRILY KICKED a chunk of snow that was on the sidewalk and watched it skitter across the icy street. He was heading away from Ruth's apartment and on his way back to the bar, cursing himself for losing control of the entire situation. She had been right to send him away.

Would it have been better if she had said yes, and they had gone to her apartment? No, that would have made things weird at work. Really, he didn't want to lose his great secretary over sex. Even though he had no idea what she did all day that made his office run so smoothly. Whatever it was, it worked.

Stopping when he got to the sidewalk, he looked at the spot where he had first held her in his arms and knew he liked this time a whole lot better. Turning, he smiled and looked at her window. The lights were blazing inside. Now that he knew it was her apartment, his eyes were drawn to it. Though the curtains were closed, he tried to see if there was a shadow of her looking back down at him.

He had to stop himself from turning back and charging up the stairs to take her into his arms so that he could see what she tasted like. Just a little taste was all he needed, though he was sure he wouldn't be able to. One taste would lead to another, and another.

Cursing, he forced himself to walk back to the bar. She had told him no, and he had to respect her for that. In fact, it made him like her a little bit more. She had the control that he lacked.

Once the warm air of the dim bar hit him, he realized he didn't want to be there. Every possible ounce of fun was gone now that Ruth was at home. It had been a fun night, watching the three women get toasted, laughing and giggling the entire time. He had a good conversation with Rafferty, who couldn't keep his eyes off the group either. When Tess Thorn had left, and the two women left got quieter, their excuses to talk to them had dried up. At about that time, Heather had started hitting on him, like every time he was in the bar since his breakup. He had no interest in the woman, but so far, she didn't take the hint.

It was during that conversation that Ruth had nearly passed out. Even now he was upset that he had taken his eye off her for one moment. It hadn't helped that Rafferty had seen it happening and had caught her. Anderson had wanted to be the one catching her. Heather had made him miss his opportunity, all for nothing.

He had to make sure she didn't pass out in the street, so he followed her out of the bar. He wasn't there for her once, and that wasn't going to happen again. But on the street, she seemed perfectly fine, if not a bit drunk.

Anderson still loved her reaction when he had questioned her about her car, and she'd realized that he knew. He loved that unexpected curse once she knew her secret was out. Her anger had almost made him laugh, but he had managed to hold it in. It wasn't even that big of a deal where she lived. He hoped she had more secrets he could find out, just to hear her curse again.

Everything that he had been thinking and feeling for the last month had bubbled to the surface as they were in that little landing, almost touching. Anderson was surrounded by the smell of roses and vanilla, and it was completely Ruth Kennedy. It was a smell he had barely noticed until one day, he recognized it. Since then, he could smell it everywhere in the office.

All he had wanted to do was kiss her, but instead, he had touched her hair, fascinated by it for what seemed like forever. Then stupidly, he asked if he could come up. Why did he ask? Of course, she said no.

If he had just carried her up the stairs, he would be stripping her down to nothing right now, tasting her lips to see if she tasted of the whiskey Cokes she had been drinking or something else that was entirely Ruth. Instead, he had asked, and she had shot him down. Which was the right call because going up there would have completely destroyed whatever they had at work, changing it all irrevocably in one night.

Mia and Rafferty were sitting at the table that the women had been sitting at earlier. They seemed to be arguing, but not like usual. More like having a friendly argument than an "I want to murder you" argument.

With them too busy to notice him, he headed for the door. He didn't need any more alcohol and didn't want to talk to anyone that was there. So instead, he slipped back out into the bitter cold. As he walked past the office, he looked up once again and saw her light still on. But instead of going up there, he got into his truck and drove away.

Now that he was away from her and could think, he knew he was not ready to lose his secretary for a little sex. Not yet, anyway.

CHAPTER 10

TUESDAY MORNING CAME TOO QUICKLY for Ruth, but at least she was not hungover. After drinking too much on Friday, she was able to rest on Saturday before book club on Sunday, which involved more drinks. Monday had actually turned out to be a reprieve as the temperatures across the state hit a record low at well minus forty, and the town actually shut down. It was a rare day that it was too cold for the citizens of Landstad to be out and about.

It had also given Ruth another day to avoid Anderson without missing a day of work and being obvious about it. What happened in the stairwell of her apartment was still fresh in her mind. Holing up in her home meant she was able to get over her hangover and pretend that nothing had happened between them until Tuesday morning.

But now the temperatures had risen to a balmy minus twenty-seven, and the town was coming alive again. Ruth was tempted to call in sick but knew he would call her out on that. He was on to her now that he knew where she lived.

Now he knew, so all her excuses could be dropped. Now she could leave her coat down in the office and not carry it back and forth every day. Sometimes she forgot it and had to go get lunch without a coat because of her mistake, and now she could just run home and get it.

With the extreme temperatures, Ruth opted for dress pants and a sweater instead of her usual skirt and blouse. When the temps were so low, the office was crazy cold, mostly in her area up front where all the big windows were, especially after three days of it being empty with the heat turned down. Anderson had complained to the building owner more than once about it, but that had fallen on deaf ears, mostly because she was the one who had to put up with the cold.

Slipping into the office, she hoped Anderson wouldn't notice she was a few minutes early. After dropping her purse on the desk, she sat down and turned on the computer. As she moved her purse to the desk drawer she kept it in, she turned on the heater she kept under her desk to warm her feet up. The flats she wore would not keep her feet warm in this cold without assistance.

"How were the roads?" came the husky voice from the adjoining office.

She turned to look at his smiling face. He thought he was so clever. "Fine."

"Grab a notepad. I think we have to write our annual letter to the building owner." Anderson waved her over.

Getting up, she grabbed the yellow legal pad she took notes on and went into his office. Sitting in the chair across from him, she set the pad on his desk so that she could write. Over the years, she had given up the pretense that she could write on her lap like a professional. She needed a hard surface when writing. "What do you want it to say this year?"

Every year, she wrote the letter, and every year, she received the letter from her rental company. Though she got a few others from her properties over the years, Anderson's was the only one that came every year without fail. Because without fail, it got cold in Landstad.

His brown eyes were on her legs, making her a little self-conscious about the pants she was wearing. "You're not wearing a skirt today."

Ruth sat up straight and squared her shoulders. "I knew it would be too cold down here to wear a skirt. I can go home and change if you need me to." She started to get up. It was an excuse to get away from him and the tension from Friday night. It was still hanging over them today.

Rising from his desk, he said, "No, don't. Just an observation, that's all. You can wear whatever you want to down here; just treat it like home. It nearly is."

Ruth lowered back into her chair, ignoring his comment about her clothes. He sat back down as she did. Picking up the pen she had set down, she nodded to the paper and asked, "What do you want to write this year?"

"Is your apartment this cold?" he questioned as his eyes went to the ceiling above them. What he didn't know was that above him was her office, not her apartment.

"It's fine. I have been there long enough to know all the quirks. Cold on the coldest days, hot on the hottest days. I usually just light the fireplace for these really cold days." She started to doodle on the paper she was holding. Anything to keep her busy and not looking at him…or thinking of him in her apartment.

"Fireplace?" His eyes snapped to her.

"Yes, it's a wood-burner, so it's really messy, but it heats the place nicely when I want it to." Her eyes were on the squiggles on her paper and not him. The fireplace was in her apartment, while her office was heated mostly by the computer equipment. It was a nice tradeoff for all the noise.

"So, we cannot get any heat, but you have a fireplace." He leaned back in his chair and folded his arms.

"Do you want me to ask for one in the letter?" She looked up for the first time and saw his eyes were watching her and not her writing.

"No, not in the letter. Did you use the fireplace all weekend?" he questioned.

"Yes, why do you ask?" She bit her lip. Was he thinking about Friday night when he wanted to go up to her apartment? Was she adding color to his fantasy? Heat rushed to her cheeks as it added color to hers.

"No reason," he mumbled.

"What do you want me to write?" she asked again, trying to get them back on topic, not that the topic was a good one.

"What did we say last year?"

"Something about this being the third year of freezing in the office and that you could rent somewhere else." Ruth remembered. It had made her a little depressed that she didn't do anything about the heating situation, but it was only an issue when the temps went below minus twenty. The first year, she had contacted a specialist, and it would take adding insulation in the walls, redoing all the interiors, and putting it all back together—thousands of dollars for a few days a year.

"Let's continue that line and say if this happens again next year, we will be looking for someplace else." He started tapping his desk with a pen as he talked.

"But where would you go?" Ruth bit her lip. She liked not driving to work. And if Anderson didn't work in her building, she wouldn't be able to write during the day as easily. If she couldn't write, what would she do? In reality, she would probably have to stop working for Anderson because this job was mostly a hobby for her.

"I was thinking this morning about Rafferty's dad's place. It is most likely better than this one."

"It's not. The apartments above the place are uninhabitable, so the offices cannot be that much better. Howard Brooks was not one for keeping up with repairs. And improvements have been nonexistent." She started doodling again. Not that she had ever been in the building —she'd bought it sight unseen and still hadn't been inside the thing. The condition didn't matter; she wanted it. She had plans.

"Is that the neighborhood gossip?" He gave her a half-smile.

She bit her lip to stop herself from grinning. "Yes, that's what we talk about at the block parties."

"Or at book club? Since most of you live on this block." He leaned back in his chair.

"I will bring it up next time." She started to doodle again on the paper.

"So, back to the letter. Anything else you can think of? Did you have anything to add?"

"No."

"You are the one affected the most; you sit out there. It is the coldest spot in the building." He peered at her legs again.

"I'm fine with it. I know that this much cold will seep in. I have been living with it for a long time now, and I will live with it for longer." Looking down at her paper, she noticed that she had spent the last few minutes just writing his name over and over again. She started to black out the name and hoped he didn't notice.

"Do you even think that the owner looks at the letter?" He leaned back in his chair again.

"Yes, I'm sure that they take all complaints seriously. Maybe there is nothing that can really be done, and they feel bad about you being cold for a few days." She crossed out the last one.

It was true; she hated for him to be uncomfortable. Over the years, she had gotten used to it, but he hadn't. She made sure that other things were fixed immediately in all her buildings, but them being cold was unfixable.

"Yeah, right. They are not even looking at the letters. Maybe I should call. I hate people like that, those who only care about the money and not the people who live and work in the buildings." Anderson was getting himself worked up about the situation.

"I don't think it will do any good to call. Let's just let it go. No use getting upset about it." She got up and left his office, throwing the entire notebook in the garbage on her way by it. She was tired of the entire situation. She knew he didn't know he was talking about her, but it hurt anyway. Was she really that callous about her properties?

"Ruth, come back," he called after her.

"No, we are done with that, Anderson." Ruth waved off his words but didn't go into his office. Sitting at her desk, she started to fiddle with the papers there, ignoring his glares.

Anderson followed her into the office and leaned against the wall. "What is wrong, Ruth?"

"I don't understand why you can't understand that it is over ninety degrees of temperature difference inside to outside. No building built over a hundred years ago can handle that. It's just how it is. I am not sending a letter that just might make the owner upset. In a few days, it will be back to normal," Ruth stated, pointing at the notepad into the garbage by her desk.

"You are just accepting it?" Anderson crossed his arms as he stared at her in confusion.

"Yes, just let it go. As you said, I am the one who is affected the most by the problem, so I will deal with it." Ruth leaned back in her chair and looked at him. He was still propped against the wall, just looking at her.

For a moment, they just stared at each other as if the first to break contact would not get their way on it. His dark brown eyes were staring at her. They were not the happy, laughing eyes that she liked; she liked them better that way.

"Why did you leave the bar on Friday?" His words took her by surprise. Where had that come from?

"No reason." Ruth didn't look away from him.

"You almost passed out in the bar." He did not look away from her.

She refused to look away first. "I can't drink a lot of alcohol. I know that."

"Isn't that what Rafferty said to you?" His eyes squinted.

"Maybe I don't listen to him." It was exactly what he had said.

He was still locked on. "Why do you hate him so much?"

Unable to look away or she would lose this battle, she said, "That is between Rafferty and me."

"Bad breakup? One-night stand?"

"Can't two people have a past together, and it not be about sex?" Watching his eyes as she said the last word, she bit her lip when they dilated a little bit.

"It's usually about sex." One eyebrow went up.

"Not this time, Anderson. Please, can we just not talk about it?" she pleaded, wanting this conversation to stop.

"Okay, one day, I will get what he did out of you. Mark my words." He pushed away from the wall and went back to his office, finally breaking eye contact with her, but she was sure that neither of them had won.

Watching him go, she knew he was not going to let it go until she finally told him, but she had never told anyone their secret, and Anderson was not going to be the first one. No matter how good he was at getting secrets from her, there were some she didn't want anyone to know.

Opening her latest book on her computer, she decided to get lost in the story she was editing. Anything to get her mind off of Rafferty. And Anderson, for that matter.

CHAPTER 11

JANUARY HAD BEEN the longest month Anderson could remember. It was almost over, and according to the weatherman, the temps were going to rise any day now. So far, they had not risen above zero in over a month—one of the coldest months on record.

The bitter cold had only lasted a week, and Ruth was back to wearing her skirts and blouses. Gone were the slacks and sweaters that she looked more comfortable in. By the end of that week, Anderson had even started wearing a sweater at work instead of his suit jacket. It made the office more relaxed.

When the frigid cold was gone, they were just left in the usual cold of a North Dakota winter. Though Anderson had been a little disappointed when the skirts came back, he realized how a nice skirt emphasized her butt and legs. Where had that been all this time? Now every time he saw her walking around the office, he couldn't take his eyes off her in hopes she would turn her back to him.

After the argument over the letter to the owner, he had invited her to eat lunch in his office. His excuse was because her office was so cold, but in reality, he wanted her closer. They had covered all kinds of topics, and now he knew her favorite color, her first car, which was the same car she still drove, and her favorite movies and TV shows.

Nothing very personal, just a light conversation about nothing, but it was something that he looked forward to every day.

After lunch, she usually went back to her desk and worked diligently until closing time. On some rare occasions, she stayed in his office after lunch, and they continued their conversations for longer. Those were the best days for Anderson. He truly enjoyed talking to her about anything.

For the first time in years, he had started to notice her as a woman and not just his personal assistant. Gone was the prickly task-orientated woman he had thought she was. Now he saw her as still very task orientated but knew that she had a quick wit and a dry sense of humor. She was sometimes hard to get laughing, but once you got her going, she didn't stop. He loved to see her slide off her glasses to ask a question or just tell him something. Who knew glasses were such a turn-on?

But through all this, he didn't make a move on her. Not that he didn't want to, but he didn't want to change their work relationship. It had not been that long since he had broken up with Daphne, and if his feelings for his personal assistant were just a rebound, he could wait for the feelings to dissipate. Unfortunately, they were not getting any better. In fact, they were getting worse.

Last week he noticed that she was typing at a fast clip for a while. He had gotten so used to it that when she stopped, he had looked over at her to see if there was an issue. There had been no issue, but she was sitting on her leg, so her bare foot peeking out at him from under her thigh. She was tapping a pencil against her mouth, and she was biting her lip. But what got him shifting in his uncomfortable seat was that she was blushing scarlet again. What was she doing?

At that point, she must have noticed she was being watched and turned to look at him, sliding her glasses down so that she could see him. The room was suddenly alive with electricity, and he almost jumped up and swept off her desk so he could lay her back on it. For some reason, he got a sense that she felt the same way at that moment because the scarlet got even darker on her skin, and she spun away from him and went back to the computer. Then she jumped up and went to the restroom.

When she came out, they didn't say a word to each other. But they never did. Not a word had been said about the night in the snowbank, nor had they talked about the near kiss in her stairway. They didn't talk about the sexual tension that hovered over them since then either. Anderson himself was ready to move their relationship forward, but he would never push Ruth if she wasn't ready.

It was late Wednesday afternoon, and Anderson looked up at Ruth, who was typing at a fast clip again, but this time with no blush. Just typing. Beyond her, he saw it had started to snow outside. Getting up, he wandered over to her part of the office to watch the flakes falling. It snowed almost every day, but today the flakes were the big fluffy ones.

Ruth turned to the window as well. "It's snowing. This is going to make my commute miserable."

Laughing at her joke, he realized she joked about where she lived more often. Well, not more often, but now he was in on the joke. It was fun being in on the joke.

"Maybe your boss should shovel you a path." He glanced at the window again. The cars parked outside their window were already covered in a white blanket of snow.

"Probably not, then I would owe him something. I wouldn't want to be in his debt." She got up from her desk to fill her coffee cup behind him.

"Yeah, you never know what he might want in return." Her smell invaded his senses as he turned to watch her, maybe get a glimpse of her butt.

Laughing as she poured, she stated, "Most likely my body."

At her words, he got to watch a scarlet blush start at the open V of her shirt and head north to her hairline. Instantly, he knew that was exactly what he would want, what he always wanted. "Fuck," he whispered under his breath.

Biting her lip, she whispered, "That too."

The sexual tension that had been hovering over them for weeks had finally descended upon them. It lay heavily as they stared into each other's eyes. Her breathing was as fast as his, but neither moved. Both were rooted to the spot, neither willing to make the first move.

Behind him, the door opened with a flurry, and someone hurried in. But he was unable to move, unable to take his eyes off the woman he was looking at. She had noticed their visitor, however, and turned towards the door.

"Mia," she gasped.

"Hey guys, what's going on?" came from the woman behind him, but he didn't turn to her.

Ruth started to talk to the waitress, but Anderson mumbled something about doing something important and went to his office. Sitting at his desk, he tried to calm down his out-of-control body and mind. Had that conversation actually happened? Had she just nearly admitted that she wanted to sleep with him?

He could hear Mia and Ruth talking in the other room. Although he could hear them clearly, he wasn't paying attention to what was being said. His mind was still on her usually icy-blue eyes that had just been heavy with desire for him. Fuck was right.

"Are you coming, Anderson?" Mia was asking, pulling him from his thoughts.

"Where?" he managed to ask.

"Were you not paying attention at all?" Mia walked into his office. "Joe Jordan is having his annual 'over the donut' party today. Are you going?"

"Never heard of it," Anderson admitted.

"She didn't either. Do you two not live in this town? Every year, the first day the temps hit zero again for the first time, Joe Jordan has a bonfire to celebrate. You know, a donut, a circle, a zero. Where have you two been hiding? Everyone knows about it. Today we hit the mark, and tonight is the party." Mia plopped down in his guest chair.

"I don't know who Joe Jordan is." Anderson did not want to go to a party. Especially one that would take place outside—it was still freezing out there.

"You don't have to know him to go to his parties, everyone is welcome. Come on, Anderson, we need a ride. My car is not starting," Mia pleaded. Her excuse was believable after the cold snap they just got throw.

"You need a designated driver?" he leaned back in his chair. Out of the side of his eyes, he saw Ruth was leaning against the doorjamb between their offices, her eyes jumping from Mia to him. Nothing about her told him if she wanted to go or not.

"Not really, but my car is out, and if Ruth goes, she doesn't have a car, so we are in need of wheels."

Turning fully to Ruth, he asked, "Are you going?"

"I don't know." Her breath was short.

"Come on, you two. Come to the party with me. I don't want to go alone!" Mia begged.

"Once you get there, you will be the center of attention." Anderson knew the woman was friends with everyone in the town. There was no way she would be alone for more than a minute.

"I will not. I promise to spend my whole night with you two. And I am not drinking too much. I am done with drinking until I pass out. It hasn't been turning out well for me for a while," Mia stated, her voice firm.

"If Ruth goes, I will drive you." Anderson turned to the woman. In reality, he wanted her alone and indoors, but if he can be with her outside drinking, that might work too. Being with her longer than eight hours a day was a plus.

Mia immediately turned her charm onto her friend, now that she had an ally. He knew it was going to work. Mia always got her way; Ruth had no chance.

Soon Ruth was agreeing, and they all had gone to get dressed warmer for the party. The temps may have hit zero degrees that day, but it was no longer that warm, if you even considered that warm. After getting on as many layers as he thought would block out the cold, he drove back to pick up the girls. They were as bundled up as he was and drove in silence, other than Mia giving directions to the bonfire.

It was dark when they got to the party, which was in full swing.

People were everywhere, and there was a giant fire blazing in the middle of it all. Only in Landstad could there be a random party, and so many people would show up.

They were each handed a beer when they arrived, and they wandered around the throngs of people, stopping every now and then so Mia could talk to someone. He was surprised by how many people he knew as they went. Many stopped and said hi or just nodded at him. Once they had been there for a while, he started to enjoy himself, or maybe it was because he was on his second beer. Mia was on her fourth and in no rush to stop despite her earlier words. Ruth was still on her first. Anderson didn't think she was even drinking it.

With Ruth close to his side, he wanted to put an arm around her. He could tell she didn't enjoy being around all the people. One day over lunch, she had told him that crowds were one of her biggest fears, crowds and snakes. At least there would be no snakes here tonight.

Someone bumped into her, sending her hard into his side. Reaching out an arm, he steadied her and then just left his arm around her. She had dropped her beer in the incident, and Anderson reached down to get it for her, but she shook her head, and he left it on the ground.

Mia turned to them with a half-drunk smile. "Isn't this great?"

"You go have fun, Mia. You don't have to babysit me." Ruth glanced around the crowd.

"I am not babysitting you, silly. I am partying with you." Mia finished her beer and pulled another from her coat pocket like a magician.

Just then, Rafferty came up behind her and pulled Mia into his arms, whispering something only she could hear. Color drained from her face, and she pushed out of his arms.

Calmly, she handed her beer bottle to Anderson and turned on Rafferty. With everything she had, she punched at him, but he dodged it, and she fell into the snow. At the last second, she grabbed his feet and pulled him to the ground too.

At that point, Anderson dropped his arm from around Ruth and handed her Mia's beer and his. The two were rolling around on the ground with Mia punching, kicking, and maybe biting, and Rafferty was just taking it and laughing. The woman could have done some real damage if her hands weren't in heavy mittens, and the man wasn't bundled against the cold. Anderson pulled the woman off him and held her around the waist so that she couldn't go back at it.

"Never, ever speak to me again. Never!" she yelled at the man still on the ground.

"I think it is time to head home," Anderson announced. Pulling Mia away from Rafferty, he hoped that Ruth would follow because he was busy keeping her friend from going back to attack his friend.

She stopped fighting him after a bit and soon, she was asking for her beer back as they walked to the car. Once there, she finished off the one she had just opened and then climbed into the back seat of the truck without incident.

"I will drive," Ruth stated after Mia shut her door.

"I didn't drink that much," he informed her.

"I don't care. I will drive. I haven't had any more than a sip." Ruth walked around the car to the driver's side.

"Don't you like beer?" Anderson asked as he got into the car on the passenger side.

"Not my drink of choice."

He handed her the keys, enjoying the idea of watching her drive his truck. She so rarely drove that he wondered if she was any good at it. Could she even drive?

Adjusting the seat and the mirror, she glanced at Mia in the back seat, and when she turned back to the front, she caught him looking at her.

"You don't think I can drive, do you?" Ruth questioned with a smile.

"Maybe."

"I can drive the pants off of you, Anderson." She winked at him and put the truck in gear.

"I hope so, Ruth." He watched her blush as she realized exactly what she'd said.

CHAPTER 12

WHAT WAS wrong with her mouth? It had gotten her into trouble all day. She knew the sexual tension was getting to her. Most days, she had daydreamed of them having sex in different areas of the office: on the desks, against the wall, in the little bathroom, in the back corner by the file cabinets, even pressed against the front window where the frost was so thick you couldn't see through it. Living out all the scenes she had written over the years, only this time it wasn't her characters; it was her and Anderson.

Except he had never even kissed her, not once. So yeah, maybe they'd come close, but that was just the one time in the stairwell, and there hadn't been a repeat of that, which had left her believing that he wasn't interested when he was sober.

That was until today. For the first time in a long time, he was interested, very interested. If Mia hadn't come in at that moment, she would have thrown herself into his arms and pushed him into that window and had her way with him. Had Mia saved her from her fantasies? Had she put a stop to what could have been a very nice evening? Or would it have just been a disaster that ruined their professional relationship?

The tension had been so thick, Ruth could almost see it. It had been the same the day he had been watching her as she was doing the final edit of the sex scene between Jessa and Link (formerly Jack). As she edited it, the scene was vivid in her mind, and she had felt his eyes on her. Looking up, she saw the desire in his eyes. She had seen the longing. She had seen that he wanted her, not Jessa, badly. Her body got out of the chair to go to him, but she regained her faculties enough to run to the bathroom instead.

And now today, those same feelings were bouncing around them again. Neither had wanted to go to the party, but both had gone in hopes of chilling the tension between them in the cold temperatures. It had not worked.

The moment she had turned onto the road, Mia had started talking about everything and anything. Apparently, she was just beyond buzzed tonight and very chatty. It was up to Anderson to try to keep up with the conversation because Ruth was concentrating on the roads. Ruth quickly realized she hadn't paid enough attention when they were coming out that she had no idea how to get back. Thankfully, drunk Mia was able to get them back to town with only a few wrong turns.

Pulling up to Mia's building, Ruth watched Anderson help Mia out of the truck and walked her to her door. When Mia went in the door, Anderson stayed to make sure she made it up the stairs and into her apartment.

Knowing she should slip away while he was busy with Mia, Ruth instead watched him helping her friend. Then Ruth turned to hurry through the snowy street to her own door across the road. It was disheartening that he didn't stop her; she thought he would have. At least, she hoped he would stop her, even if she had bolted while he was busy.

She had made it to the top of the stairs when the door opened behind her. Anderson. Spinning around, she looked at him standing at the landing below her.

His eyes bored into hers. "Can I come up?"

"For sex?" She needed to know. It was what she wanted, but not what they needed. Not yet.

"No, just to talk." He smiled and took one step up.

"Are you sure?" She didn't move as he took another step up.

He pulled off his mittens and took another step up. "Yes, just talk."

"Because we are not there yet." She watched him slide off his hat, leaving his hair half standing on end, and took another step towards her.

"I know, Ruth." Another step.

"Just so you know," she whispered as he got to the last step before the one she was on.

"Can I come up, Ruth?" he whispered as he looked into her eyes.

"Yes," she whispered back to him. Turning, she walked up the last two steps, stopping as she took off her coat and shoes in the hallway. Then she tucked the mittens and hat on a shelf above the coat rack. Anderson followed her lead. When their outerwear was neatly put away in the hallway, she opened the door to her apartment. It was not locked; it almost never was.

Quickly, she scanned the room to see what he would see when he saw the place. She had few guests, but since the book club started to meet there, she had started to see it differently. All the furniture had been purchased when she had moved into the place. Even though she had a say in what she and Franky bought, it was more his style than hers. But since it wasn't broken or worn out, she kept it. Large, comfortable furniture in shades of blue and green. Looking at it from Anderson's eyes, it looked old and worn.

All except the chef's kitchen she had installed the year before he moved to town. When she had complained to Frank that the appliances were not working well, he decided to just redo the outdated kitchen. She loved it still to this day, even though she didn't cook much, preferring to eat her big meal at lunch and having just a light supper.

"This is not what I expected," Anderson said from behind her.

"What were you expecting?" she wondered as she pulled the bun from her hair. It was always the first thing to go when she arrived home from work. She loved the ritual of removing it.

"Less hardwood, stainless steel, and granite." He was not looking at the kitchen anymore, he was watching her.

"The kitchen got a good makeover a few years ago, and it turned out nice. But I hate cooking, so maybe it was wasted on me." She looked away from him and over at the kitchen.

"You seem like the type that loves to cook." Anderson looked back to the kitchen again as he sat down on a stool at the island.

"Have I ever brought treats or lunch to work?"

"Not that I remember." He chuckled at the answer.

"I eat a big lunch so that I don't have to come home and cook. I eat my ham sandwich at night," she reminded him of the sandwich he always ordered.

"So, you won't bring cookies to work?"

"No, I do not share cookies." She laughed at his expression of pain. "Do you want to listen to some music?"

"Sure, what kind do you have?"

"Every kind. I pay for a music service, so I have access to every-thing commercial-free." Pulling out her phone, she opened the app and looked up at him.

"Country?" he questioned.

"Any?" She knew that she could pick from many different kinds.

"Today's."

"Okay," she said, typing in the station. Then she saw him jump when the speakers that were placed around the room started to play a song. Maybe it was a little loud. "Sorry."

She turned down the speakers with her phone before setting it down on the counter. She had bought the system for her office, but the speakers were no match for the fans that kept her equipment cool. It had only taken her a day to switch back to the noise-canceling headphones she wore. With nowhere else to put the system, she put it in her apartment. Now she couldn't live without it.

Anderson picked up her phone, looked at it for a minute, then looked at the speakers around the room. As he put her phone back down, he said, "You have good taste in music systems."

"Thank you. I like music. This gets more use than the TV most weeks."

"I think I should run some speakers down to the office so we can enjoy music during the day." He got up and took her hand and pulled her into his arms. "Dance?"

She put her arms around his neck, and they slow danced around the kitchen. Loving the feel of his arms around her, she wanted to rest her head against his chest but didn't want him to think she was leading him on. They should only be talking tonight. When the song ended, she reluctantly pulled out of his arms.

"I have to go take some layers off."

"So, it's not me making you hot?" He tucked a wayward hair behind her ear.

Biting her lip to stop her smile, she said, "Nope, just too many layers."

He was laughing when she walked away from him. Once in her room, she leaned against the door and just breathed for a few minutes. Anderson was in her house, and he danced with her in the kitchen. Anderson.

Shedding all her layers of clothing, she pulled on an old Landstad Tigers sweatshirt in black and orange school colors and black leggings. She was desperate not to look too nice for him—she really did only want to talk. She was just too nervous to do anything else. It had been a dozen years since she had done any of that stuff. Outside of her head, that is.

When she came back into the living room, she didn't see Anderson anywhere. He must have left. Her heart sank.

Deciding that's what had happened, Ruth went to turn off the music still playing from the speakers around the room, depressed at how the night had ended. Just as she picked up her phone to turn off the music, she saw him emerge from the bathroom, holding a pile of clothes. "I thought I would shed a few layers also."

Now he was wearing just the jeans he had changed into and a gray long-sleeve T-shirt. Setting his other clothes on the table by the door, he walked over to her in the kitchen. He took her hand and led her to the couch.

"Let's talk. That's what I got invited up here for." He sat down and turned to face her, warming her heart because he wasn't pushing her. Talking could mean so much in the beginning of a relationship, and Ruth knew that most of the time, it meant sex.

Sitting down at the other end of the couch, she turned to him and said, "What do you want to talk about?"

"You," he said, reaching out and taking her hand in his. He scooted over on the couch so that they were closer.

"I am not interesting."

"You, Ruth, are fascinating. Lately, every day holds a new discovery about you."

"Like what?" She narrowed her eyes at him.

Ruth wondered what he could possibly find interesting in their lunch conversation. She loved them, but he wasn't as interested in her as she was in him.

"Like the fact that your stereo system costs more than my yearly car insurance bill." He looked over at the nearly hidden speakers.

"You should talk to your insurance guy; you are paying too much," she joked, wondering if he knew how much she paid for the system. It had been more expensive than she liked, but in the end, she loved having them and enjoyed them every day.

"His personal assistant says he is too busy." He squeezed the hand he was still holding.

"She sounds awful." Ruth bit her lip to stop the smile.

"She's very nice." He rested his arm on the back of the couch and touched a lock of her hair. "How long have you lived up here?"

Sighing, she said, "Twelve years this summer."

"Does anyone live across the hall? Since you leave your coats and boots in the hallway."

"No, that one is mine also. I like my privacy." She noticed the shades were closed. With her free hand, she grabbed her phone and opened them with an app.

"Privacy when you want it?" He watched the shades go up, but then his eyes came back to her.

"Yes," she admitted, realizing that it had started to snow again.

"Why do you stay? Why not buy a house? Move away from town?"

"Let's see. It's complicated, my mom, and I don't want to mow the yard." She smiled as she answered,

"Complicated? Do you like it here?"

"Some of it. I like my job. I like the book club. I like that I don't need to drive. I also like the predictability of the town. I know Mia will be at the café all the time, I know the ladies at the bank, and I know when celebrations are. I know that when Luke Wyatt comes in, the football team needs donations, that when snow starts to pile up in town, kids will start playing on that snow hill once school is out. Predictability." She leaned her head against the back of the couch and tucked her foot under her leg.

"What don't you like about it?" His fingers were still playing with her hair.

"That everybody knows my business, and I know all of theirs. A few months ago, if you told me I would be going to a party with Mia Lawson, I would have called you a liar. I still don't really believe it."

"You and Mia were not friends? But you went to the café every day."

"I did, I do. We were acquaintances. We know a lot about each other, but we didn't know each other very well. Growing up in a small town is like that. How many kids did you graduate with?"

"Around three hundred and fifty."

"I graduated with twenty-four, eighteen of which had been there since kindergarten." It had been twelve years, and she could tell you the six that had come later and when they had arrived.

"Was Rafferty one of them?" he asked.

"Yes, your friend Rafferty was in my class. We are only a week apart in age. He is older." She remembered that her mom always sent a cake for treats for her birthday and Rafferty always claimed them as his. Now looking back, she realized it was because his own mother hadn't ever any treats.

"Is Mia your age?"

"No, Mia is younger by a year and a half, but two in school. So, you had so many kids in your class, and you didn't know many of them. I knew them all for years before I graduated. Mia was a cheerleader, and Rafferty played sports."

"Did they hang out together back then?"

"No, not really. I hung out more with Rafferty than Mia ever did in high school."

"Wait. You and Rafferty were friends in high school?" he asked in confusion.

She laughed at his reaction. "Yes, we were both a part of the same friend group. I have many fond memories of young Rafferty."

"So, were you a ballplayer? Cheerleader? Nerd?" Smiling, he settled back into the couch.

"None of the above. I was a girlfriend. I did everything Franky did, and nothing he did not. I was pretty dull," she mumbled, feeling ashamed of the stupidity of her youth.

"How long did you date him?"

"Six years."

She saw his eyes widen. "I thought you broke up at around eighteen?"

"Nineteen, so maybe it was seven years. We started dating when we were twelve. Never broke up until the end." She sighed.

"Do you still love him?"

"No, not anymore. It took a while; my life was wrapped up in him for a long time. It was hard to get it untangled." Many years of her life had been wasted on him.

"Do you know where he is?"

"Yes, Bismarck, married with three kids. Frank moved to be closer to him. Maybe he has another kid now. I don't know." Once Frank was gone, her connection to him was gone as well.

He nodded. "Did you go to college?"

"No, I didn't have the grades to get in."

"How did you not have good grades? You are the most studious person I know. You are always working on something at your desk," he stated.

Once again, she felt ashamed that she didn't do a lot of work for him. For years she had spent her work hours editing her books. She vowed she would stop soon.

"Different skill set, working in an office I have worked at for years. I barely graduated from school. I wouldn't have if I hadn't been in Landstad." She shrugged, hating to actually admit it.

He looked confused. "Why?"

"Because no place else would have let me graduate." She bit her lip, not wanting to get into her past.

The principal had all but told her that when she was actually graduating. He had been nice about it and had been very understanding, but he had also told her that her chances of getting into a college were nonexistent. At the time, she didn't care. Later she wished she had tried anyway, for herself more than anything.

"No, why did you barely graduate?" He squeezed her hand as he asked.

"I was sick a lot the last few years of high school, so I missed a lot of school." She looked at their hands, not at him.

"But you never miss work." It was the truth—she never used her sick leave from work. She usually never even got sick, not anymore.

"I was born with a birth defect that affected my kidneys. By high school, one had failed, and the other was failing. I had a transplant the year after I graduated, so I am better now. Well, I have only one kidney, but I'm better compared to how I was before that." She hated to tell people that she was weak. Staying in Landstad meant she rarely ran into anyone who didn't know.

"I never would have guessed."

"I always thought that Frank liked me because I spent so much time laying on his couch watching TV with him. He would sit in his recliner, and we would make fun of the people on the screen. Franky hated watching TV with his dad. I loved it. I only had Chester in my life, and he was a drunk, so it was fun to have something of a dad in Frank. And I was sort of daughter to him." She smiled at the memory.

"So, you would go to your boyfriend's house when you were sick and watch TV with his dad?" Anderson asked in disbelief.

"You make it sound weird. I lived there for two years. His parents were like my parents."

"You lived with your teenage boyfriend and his parents?" His fingers stopped touching her hair.

"From sixteen to just after graduation, then we moved in here." She looked around at the apartment. It hadn't changed much since then, except the kitchen, and she wished she had somehow made it more of her own since then.

"I thought your mom was super religious? She let her daughter live in sin?" he questioned.

"I said I was doing it, and she didn't say no. She had been married to Chester for two years by then, and we did not get along. It was easier for me not to be in the house." The fights had stopped between them, and so far, they hadn't arisen again. But since then, Chester had stopped drinking, and she had become an adult.

"Then you moved in here with him?"

She wondered what he was thinking. Even at the time, it had been weird living with Franky and his parents. But it had been so much better than her mom's house. It had been her chance to see what being in a real family was like.

"Yes, I started working for his dad to make money for a house and other stuff when he graduated. He dumped me in April, not long after the transplant, for the woman he married. They had been dating since late September. Most people in town don't know about the transplant and thought I was hiding because of the scandal of the breakup. But it took a long time to get better, longer than I had expected. Then I just started back here because Frank wanted me to still work for him." She laid her head back down.

"Did you ever think about leaving?" His fingers skimmed over the shell of her ear.

"No, for a few years I was convinced he would come back to me, to what we had. We had a good thing. When he got married, I had to let that idea go. He wasn't coming back to me. By then, I was settled into my rut, and I have stayed in that rut."

"I am glad I am a part of that rut." He smiled at her.

"Enough about my sad life. Tell me about Andy." She laughed at the sound of his nickname. "Anderson."

He winked at her. "What do you want to know, Angel?"

"Did you get to live with your girlfriend in your parent's house?" She was not getting into it about her nickname. *Ignore it, and he will stop*, she hoped.

"I never even got to stay in the same room when I brought a girl-friend home for the holidays in college."

"A shame. Who did you bring home?"

When he didn't say anything, she wondered if he would answer. Had she asked too much? She had told him so much about herself; had it been too much to ask?

"Her name was Noel, and I thought I loved her. It was during my senior year of college."

"What happened?" She wanted to know who could still make him sound sad.

"How do you know something happened?" He raised one eyebrow in question.

"Because you have no spouse named Noel."

"What happened was my brother decided that he wanted her, and he got her. They have been married for seven years." Ruth knew that there was more to the story than that but didn't want to push.

"Your own brother? I didn't think brothers were like that." How painful for him.

"Brothers are not supposed to be like that," he agreed.

"How about Daphne? What happened there?" She bit her lip. She had been someone they barely talked about for years. Though he lived with her, he never talked about her, never brought her up. But then they weren't this close before. And since he had informed her of the breakup months ago, she had been scared to ask but dying to know. Because who would actually dump Anderson? No sane person, that was who.

"I met Daphne when I was looking for a house about five years ago. She sold real estate. I didn't end up buying a house because, within a few months, my father shipped me out here. But when I moved here, I moved some of my stuff to her place, and on the weekends, I would stay with her. At the time I was only supposed to be here for two years tops, but my dad doesn't think that I would be good at this in a bigger market like Grand Forks. So, I get the Landstad branch."

"Where is your brother?" she asked.

Anderson smiled turned brittle. "In the office right next to my dad. He was born ready for a larger market. In fact, he is my boss."

"His name is Jonathan, right? The Jonathan that calls every once in a while?" How many times had he called, and she had just thought he was someone from his dad's office? She never would have thought he was Anderson's brother.

"Yes."

"So, what happened with Daphne? You didn't finish. You were supposed to be here for two years and..." She pulled her feet under her on the couch. Her head was still leaning against the back of the couch into his touch. She loved him touching her.

"And I asked her to marry me. I was tired of the long distance. If she would move, which she never wanted to, I would try harder to get back. Maybe if my dad saw that I was in a serious relationship, he would move me back." His eyes were so sad.

"She said no?" Ruth couldn't believe that there was a woman out there that would say no to Anderson.

"Yes, and then she told me that I was the second Miles brother to ask her to marry her that week. Apparently, she had been seeing Jonathan for a few months, and he was going to leave Noel for her. I didn't tell her that my brother would never leave Noel—my father would disown him. Noel is the perfect daughter-in-law," he finished bitterly.

"Your brother has stolen two of your girlfriends? Makes me glad my mother only had one child. Siblings don't sound like as much fun as I had always imagined." She hated that his brother would do something like that to him.

"I sometimes wish I had a sister instead of a brother," he said.

"Do you still love her?" She didn't want to know the answer right now.

"I miss what we had, what we could have had," he said, though she noticed he didn't answer the question.

Pushing aside her disappointment, she changed the subject to something less heartbreaking. "Are you still wanting to leave? Go back to Grand Forks?"

"I don't know. I don't want to work with Jonathan, and he is there, but I still kind of want to be there." He looked out the window at the snow still falling in the streetlights.

"It's more fun in the city."

"My biggest issue might be convincing my personal assistant to go with me." He leaned his head onto the couch and looked at her.

"She is stuck in her rut here in Landstad," she replied with a smile.

"Then I am going to have to try to get her unstuck."

"I won't leave Landstad, Anderson," she sighed and stated the truth. She had accepted it years before. This was her home.

His smile faltered for a moment before he said, "You sound pretty convinced that nothing will make you leave."

"People in this town may know my past, present, and future, but I am home here. I have my work, my job, friends, and my mom here. My world is here, and unless that world crumbles, I will be here," she admitted, knowing that if her secrets came out, she would have to leave. There were things in her life she didn't want everyone to know about, things she liked to keep to herself.

She looked down at their hands still linked together on the couch. The small contact was enough to make her relaxed and comfortable with him. When his thumb played with her hand, it sent shivers down her spine.

Without looking up at him, she asked, "Why are you here?"

"With you? Because I find you fascinating. I want to find out more about you."

"You have known me for four years now. I was there the entire time."

"I think I didn't see you before because I was in a relationship that I was loyal to. When I moved here, it was early in the relationship. I wasn't looking at other women. Over the years, you became my personal assistant, trusty Ruth. I never looked beyond that. Then one day I saw you, and it was like I opened my eyes, and you were there. I have been thinking about you for months. Wanting you for months." He brushed his hand over her cheek.

"It seems sudden."

"It hit me one day. It was instant."

"What about my job? I like my job."

"You will always have a job."

"Is it only about sex?"

"No, I want to talk to you for hours. I want to see the world through your eyes. I want to get to know everything about you."

"The last time I was in a relationship, I was shattered when it ended. I put everything into that man, and he walked away from everything I was offering him. I don't know if I can let that happen again."

"I understand. I will have to deal with learning to trust, trust that you will be faithful to me."

"Are you willing to put in the time needed for a relationship to build around our issues? Date maybe, make out maybe, find out more about each other before jumping into bed together and ruining everything? Can we go slow and see if there is something here?"

"I think that is a great idea. Can we go out on Friday night?"

"No."

"Shooting me down already?" He looked away from her then.

"I go to my mother's on Fridays. Anytime during the week would be good, though." She wondered if she had missed her chance to see if this was going to be something.

"How could I forget your mom?" His eyes returned to her.

"Because you haven't met her."

"Tomorrow night? I will walk you home and cook dinner."

"Yes," she said, maybe a little too eagerly.

"Good. I should get going so that I can plan our date."

Getting up, they walked to the door and into the hallway. Sliding his shoes on, he grinned at her as he pulled her into his arms. "Can I kiss you tonight?"

"If you want." She felt a shiver run through her entire body at his touch.

"Want," he whispered as his mouth touched hers lightly. She felt him slide his hand into her hair and pulled her head so that their lips pressed firmly together. Before she was able to get used to the feeling and pull him closer to deepen the kiss, he pulled away from her, leaving her standing at the top of the stairs as he started down them. As she watched him walk down the stairs, he turned at the bottom and said, "Good night, Ruth."

CHAPTER 13

WHY HADN'T he dated anyone who worked in the office before? It was amazing. In the beginning, he had thought it was going to be awkward, that was until Ruth opened her mouth. Personal assistant Ruth was very different from girlfriend Ruth, and girlfriend Ruth was now his personal assistant. He had never known that she held back a lot of her personality at work.

True to their conversation, they had taken it slowly. As February progressed, they had gotten to know each other. They made supper together, though she did really hate to cook, so they ended up going out to every restaurant within a fifty-mile radius and always ended the evening making out on her couch. Or in the car or in her entry-way. So far, they had not progressed further than that.

Even though she had hinted at it the night of their talk, it had taken a few dates for it to sink in for Anderson. There hadn't been anyone in her bed since Franky walked out when she was nineteen. She was nervous about them sleeping together. There was a little frustration on his part, but for Ruth, he would wait as long as she needed. He would in no way push her—she was too special for that.

Looking up from his computer, he saw her with a pencil in her mouth, reading glasses on, and staring at her computer screen. She must have felt his eyes on her because she turned and slid her glasses down her nose and looked at him.

"What?" she asked in confusion.

"Just looking at you," he admitted, leaning back in his chair.

"Well, you should wait for after work for those thoughts." She winked at him.

He grinned. "How do you know what I was thinking?"

"You're a guy; it's all you think about." She was right.

"I will stop…for now. What are we doing tonight?" he asked, as he did every day. Only on the weekends when she went to her mom's house and book club night did they not spend the evening together.

"I don't know. Maybe make something upstairs?"

"How about my place?" So far, she had not been to his place, but she preferred her's. He did too, but he liked his place also and wanted her to see who he was and how he lived.

"Then you will have to drive me back here and then drive home. At my place, you can just drive home." She applied her logic, which she had told him more than once.

"Or I could just stay all night at your place." He winked at her.

"Anderson," she warned.

"Okay." He let it go. "How about I get pizza, and we can watch a movie?"

"Sounds fun, then we can neck a little." She laughed and got up to get more coffee.

He closed his eyes. He loved the teasing and the joking that she was doing constantly. Where had that been for the last four years? The first day after the bonfire, she had started not being as guarded about what she said; she just let what came to her mind out. From side comments about herself or him to sexual banter, it had taken time to realize how much she had been holding back.

"Taking a nap?" she asked from somewhere close.

Snapping his eyes open, she was standing so close to him that he was not convinced that they were not touching. Reaching out, he pulled her onto his lap. He had never done this before in the office, but she was so close he couldn't help himself. He had to touch her.

She willingly went into his arms. Her skirt rode up high on her thighs as she scooted closer to him. He ran his hands from her hips up to her breasts, relishing the feel of her breast in his hands. With her hands linking behind his neck, she pulled him towards her. Meeting her eager lips with a matching vigor, his hand slid away from her breasts to her back so he could pull her closer to him.

Over the past few weeks, their relationship had maybe not progressed into the bedroom, but they had definitely spent many hours kissing and touching.

His heart was pounding in his chest, and his erection was pressed firmly into her core as he pulled away from the kiss, panting. He had pulled away, but she had just turned her attention to his ear and was licking it. When she took the lobe into her mouth and sucked on it, he gently pushed her away. "No, we can't do that here. Remember, professional down here."

Disappointment and hurt flashed in her ice-blue eye as she climbed off his lap. Without a word, she went back to her desk. She didn't even look at him as she sat down, just turned her attention to her computer.

Shit, he had hurt her feelings. But anyone could have walked in and seen her on his lap. Or was it that he wanted to be inside her, and she kept pushing him away? Was this some sort of payback on his part?

Most people in town knew that they were dating by now. Even Rafferty had mentioned it when they met for drinks last Friday. Oddly, he had taken on the role of father or something and told Anderson he had better treat her right. She deserved good things. Rafferty hadn't pushed for details about their relationship, even though Rafferty was always quick with the details about his conquests.

"I am going to get lunch," Anderson announced. A few minutes in the mid-February cold would do him good. Cool down his body a little.

Without grabbing a jacket, he walked out the door without waiting for her answer. Slowly, he walked across the road to the café. Mia was behind the counter in a bright red shirt, and her hair was now pink.

"Happy Valentine's Day, Anderson. Do you have big plans for Ruth tonight?" Mia was bubbly today.

Panic rushed through his body, panic and fear. He had forgotten about Valentine's Day. He had just suggested they have a frozen pizza and watch a movie on Valentine's Day. Their first one together.

"By that reaction, I see you have no plans. Did you forget? You can't forget, it's Ruth." Ruth's best friend, had written their order without asking and handed it to the kitchen as she lectured him.

"I forgot." He sunk down on a stool.

"Anderson, it's your first Valentine's Day as a couple. Did you get her anything at all?" Mia leaned against the counter in interest.

"No." How was he supposed to show her she was special if he forgot a major holiday? The first holiday since they got together.

"No card, no nothing?" Mia quirked an eyebrow as she reminded him how easy this holiday could be. In fact, last year he had gotten Daphne roses and taken her out for dinner and dancing. This year he had forgotten, and Ruth deserved to be treated better than Daphne ever had.

"I forgot."

"What are we going to get her? In Landstad today?" She pondered out loud as she looked out the picture window at the snowy street beyond.

"I don't know. I messed up…again." He admitted.

"Again?" Mia questioned.

"I hurt her feelings this morning. I should have been nicer but wasn't." He hoped she didn't ask more about what happened.

"How about giving her a day off? She was saying she doesn't get a lot of alone time lately? I think she kind of misses being alone. You can still see her in the evening, but she can spend the day doing what Ruth does." Mia said, getting a little excited about the plan as she talked.

"I will think about it. Thanks." She had handed him the boxes containing their lunches. On the way out of the café, he glanced at the menu board to see what Ruth actually got, in case she asked.

With a quick walk across the road, he pushed open the office door and walked in, but the room was quiet, too quiet. Something was off. Ruth was gone. Setting down the boxes on her desk, he checked the back room and the bathroom. She was gone.

His heart sank. He had messed up, and she was mad at him. She had never left before when she was mad, which was rare, but in those times, she always just stewed at her desk. The only other time she had left was when Rafferty had shown up.

As he was wondering what he should do, he got a text.

Ruth: Have a headache, taking the rest of the day off. Sorry, I have to cancel tonight too.

Anderson walked over to his desk and sat down heavily in the chair. Should he go up there and apologize? Should he let her sulk about it? Work relationships were hard. He should have just kept on kissing her, letting it go as far as it goes. Feeling her pressed against him, her mouth on his.

Tossing the phone on his desk, he noticed a piece of bright yellow paper in the middle of his desk, a note from Ruth's little book she used to write down his messages. She rarely used it since he was usually in the office. It said:

Daphne wants a call back. She said you know the number. Said to tell you she loves you and Happy Valentine's Day.

She didn't sign it, but Anderson knew her writing. Crumpling it up, he threw it in the garbage where his relationship with Daphne already was. Had been for months. A note like this wouldn't change anything.

Ruth, such a professional that she had written everything down for him, even if it hurt her. Did she think he was seeing Daphne again? She must, with how the message was written.

Getting up, he left the lunches on the desk as he left the office.

Opening her door, he wondered about knocking since she rented the entire floor and used it as her own. Was he intruding when he walked past her shoes on the floor? The ones she had worn today were there.

He called her name as he knocked on the door, but she didn't answer. Knowing he had to talk to her, he opened the door and was surprised that it wasn't locked. Walking into her apartment without her was eerie, and he could feel that she wasn't there. Her presence was missing from the rooms. In her bedroom, the clothes she had been wearing today were on the bed. Not folded like always, just thrown on it.

Since they had started dating, he knew that she changed clothes the moment she walked in the door of her apartment. Now she had already changed today, but he didn't know if she had put on jeans to go out or leggings to stay in. There were no signs in the apartment as to where she could have disappeared to.

Mia would maybe know, he thought, even if he had just seen her a few minutes before. Back in the hallway, he pulled on his shoes. His eye caught sight of the door to her storage apartment. It had made him chuckle that she rented a storage apartment, but since her own apartment had no clutter, he figured she kept stuff in there.

Walking to the door, he tried the nob, but it was locked. At least she locked one of her doors. But where was she?

After talking to Mia at the café, Mandy at the clinic, Tess at the bank, and the lady at the library, he had run out of people to talk to and places to check. Mia had said she would watch the office for signs that her mother was picking her up or signs that she had returned.

How could he talk to her if he couldn't find her?

CHAPTER 14

LOOKING through the fridge for something to eat, Ruth opted for a peanut butter sandwich. Her fridge was sadly close to empty. Once the sandwich was made, she leaned on the counter to eat while she looked through her texts, all twelve of them.

Some were from the book club, which she responded to. There was also a group one that said book club was on for tomorrow. The other six were from Anderson. Those she ignored, not wanting the relationship they'd had to end with a text. Because that was what he was going to do, whether in a text or in person, it didn't matter. It was over. Daphne wanted him back.

When she had made it home from the office after the call from Anderson's ex, she had been in tears. After shedding her clothes and changing into sweats and a T-shirt, she had locked herself in her office—not the bed she wanted to bury herself into.

Forcing herself to stop thinking of Anderson, she had put on her noise-canceling headphones and lost herself in a love story that was going to work out in the end. The hero was smart, charming, and madly in love with the heroine. It was a story and nothing like real life. Today, all she wanted was the fantasy, throwing herself into the story until her stomach had made her stop typing. At least she had been able to block out everything for hours.

At that point, it had been in the early morning hours after her first and last Valentine's Day with Anderson. It was then that she called her mom and told her she would not be going to the farm this weekend. Then she had ignored all of Anderson's texts and sent him a message saying she would not be in the office that day, which was Friday, giving her a weekend alone. She'd lied about being sick, which wasn't a lie at all. Her heart was sick. It counted.

After that, she had done something she never thought she would do. She contacted her rental agency and asked if there were any apartments open in Grand Forks. It was a possibility since she wasn't the only apartment owner they worked for. There was an opening, and she had told them she wanted it empty for her. For the first time in her life, she was considering moving away from Landstad.

Now that her relationship with Anderson was over, her job would be over, and her happiness would be over. Sunday, she would tell the book club that she was leaving. Then she would use the weekend to go down and clean her desk out. Monday, she would turn in her two weeks' notice, and since she had over two weeks of vacation, she would be done.

That had been a day ago, she was sure. Between writing and sleeping, she wasn't keeping track of time. Time didn't matter anymore anyway.

The new song in her headphones was a fast and fun one she had always enjoyed. Turning up the volume, she hoped it would improve her mood as she finished her sandwich. She decided to get a pop and chips for the evening and headed back to her office.

Movement caught her eye, and Anderson was standing in the doorway of her apartment. For a moment, she regretted not locking the door but realized it was better to get this over with now. She had been putting it off long enough as it was.

His lips were moving, but she couldn't hear what he was saying because of the headphones still on her head, still blaring her music.

Frozen in her spot, she clenched the chips bag and can to her chest, just watching him stalk towards her. For two days, she hadn't even tried to control the tears, letting them fall whenever her heart hurt too much to keep them in. Now she didn't want him to see how the end of their relationship was affecting her. As he drew close, she backed up until the cabinets stopped her retreat.

Taking a deep breath, then another one, she gently put the items in her arms on the counter beside her. She then pulled off her headphones and put them on the counter. In reality, she wanted to throw it all on the floor and start yelling at him for leading her on, for using her until the one he loved wanted him back. For breaking her heart.

Instead, she calmly said, "Hello, Anderson."

"Where have you been? I have been looking for you for two days," he demanded angrily, still in his winter jacket and snowy shoes.

"I have been here." She waved her hand around the mostly dark room, except for the kitchen light that she usually left on.

"Try another story, Ruth," he replied sharply. "I have been here looking for you many times. I have been calling you, but you aren't even answering your phone."

She almost looked at her phone so that she could tell him he hadn't called, but she stopped herself. He had called and texted, but she had just ignored it. All of it. But what was she supposed to do, answer and hear him tell her their little fling was over? That they were going to go back to just working together? She couldn't do that again, not after getting to know him. It was too late to go back.

"I will turn in my two weeks' notice on Monday. I have enough vacation time to cover that." Even saying the words hurt her, but not as much as him telling her they were over.

"What are you talking about?" He sounded confused by her revelation.

"Anderson, we both knew I would have to leave when this was over. And now it's over. Don't worry, I will not bother you or her." *Just breathe,* she demanded herself. *Don't let him see you fall apart.*

"You think that I want Daphne back? You think I would leave the moment she called and wanted me back?" he said, taking a step closer to her.

"You love her." Ruth shook her head, trying to hold the tears in.

His hands pushed the hair from her face and forced her to look at him. "I don't love her, Ruth. I thought I loved her once, but not anymore."

She tried not to look into his eyes. She didn't want to see his true feelings. "But it's been over two weeks, and you haven't made a move. And you pushed me away when I did. I knew it was over before she called. You aren't interested in me, not like that anymore."

"That's not true. I wanted to give you time. You needed time, and I am willing to wait for you, as long as it takes." Smiling, he brushed his thumbs against her wet cheeks.

"I thought you weren't interested anymore. I knew you would tire of me after a while. Everyone does. It was just quicker than I ever thought it would be," she whispered, admitting her worst fears to him.

Brushing a kiss across her lips, he whispered back, "I am anything but tired of you, Ruth. I want you in my bed as much today as the day we talked about it. No, that's wrong. I want you more than I did then."

"Me too." She grabbed his jacket and pulled him to her, pressing her lips fully to his. Giving in to him, she felt his tongue run over her bottom lip. She didn't hesitate to tilt her head and match his every movement. She ran her hands up his chest and into his hair so that she could hold his mouth to hers, feeling his hand slide up under her T-shirt until they cupped her bare breasts. Never was she so glad she chose to not wear a bra. A shiver ran through her at the touch.

"We need to stop, or I won't be able to," he said as his mouth left hers to place soft, open-mouthed kisses on her neck.

"No, don't stop. Don't ever stop, Anderson." She could hear the pleading in her voice, but she didn't care. She needed him.

His response was a growl as he continued to kiss and suckle along her collarbone while his fingers brought her nipples to peaks. Needing more, he quickly lifted her shirt over her head and smiled down at her in appreciation. Her hands were still in his hair, so she pulled his head down so that he could take a nipple into his mouth.

She let her head fall back as she groaned.

"Are you sure, Ruth?" Anderson asked again, his fingers and mouth making her body tingle as he touched her, tasted her. When she only nodded, it was all the answer he seemed to need. "Should we move this into the bedroom?"

"Yes, Anderson, please."

His hands slid under her butt and lifted her to him. Her legs wrapped tightly around him as he carried her across her apartment and into the bedroom, where he set her on her feet at the end of the bed. For a moment, she wondered what he thought of her bedroom; he had never been in the room before.

As if to prove her point, he kissed her deeply, his entire focus on her as she unzipped his jacket. Pushing it off his shoulders, she kissed him back. Anderson struggled to get his shoes off as they kissed, but she was rewarded by the sounds of shoes hitting the floor, followed by the polo shirt he had been wearing.

When the shirt was gone, he looked back at her with a grin, maybe because she was shirtless, and her breasts were right there. But she was sure he wasn't just looking at them. He was looking at her. With care, he nudged her until she was on the bed, and as she scooted back to the center, he followed her.

After settling in beside her, he ran a delicate trail of kisses across her breasts before looking up at her and kissing her lips again. But this time with the passion that promised what was coming next.

With his hands cupping her breasts again, he growled into her mouth before tearing himself away as he reached under him. From under his back, he pulled the now wrinkled clothes she had worn to work two days before that were still on the bed. He held them up a moment before tossing them onto the floor. Pulling her back into his arms, he nuzzled her neck and announced, "I will find out where you spent the last two days, soon."

"Do you want to discuss that now?" She giggled, but his only answer was to lean away from her and push the sweatpants she wore down her hips and off her legs.

"No." Anderson's eyes were on the newly exposed skin, and his words were barely a whisper as his hands skimmed up her legs.

She wished there was a little less light, but it was streaming in through the windows, leaving no shadows as his mouth blazed a hot trail down her body. She laid back and let him take charge; it had been forever. But she didn't think Franky had ever made her body tingle with just a touch of his lips. At least she couldn't remember it happening, and she was sure she would've remembered that.

Making fast work of his jeans, she pushed them down his narrow hips as his hands worked her breasts, quickly replaced by his mouth. Suddenly she was impatient to see him, all of him, even what his gray boxer briefs hid. It had been forever since she had been with a man, but it was coming back to her quickly. Her body definitely remembered what it liked, even if she hadn't done this in years.

When his fingers skimmed her clit, she stopped altogether. All focus was on his movements. There was no doubting herself and what she was doing. Instead, she let her body respond to his touch, not caring about the moans that escaped her lips. Or when his mouth took over, and she had to grasp the comforter below her, or how she screamed of pleasure. Over and over again.

Ruth had written this type of scene over and over again over the years, but never once did she imagine she could feel like a character in her books. The pleasure she was feeling was not how sex had been before. Franky had never made her feel like this.

She was spent, unable to even move as he kissed his way back up her body. At this point, she didn't know how she was going to return the favor, no matter how much she wanted to.

"That was worth the wait," he whispered as he rained kisses on her breasts.

Arching her back, she regretted the time lost. "We should have done this weeks ago."

"It wouldn't be this good if we hadn't waited." His voice was husky as his hard erection pressed into her stomach.

Her energy was instantly back, and she wanted him now. Wrapping her legs around him, she rolled him onto his back. Whatever he was going to say next was lost in a groan as she shimmied down his body, pressing and kissing as she went. His hard erection was between them the entire time.

Kissing her way down his chest, she grinned at him when she looked up to see him watching her, his eyes hooded and his breathing shallow as she took him into her hand. From what she remembered, he was far larger than Franky had been. And when she slipped his head between her lips, she was sure he was. Not that she was complaining, just needing to adjust.

It had been years, but based on the guttural sounds he was making, she was doing everything right. Or at least close enough that he was enjoying it. As she licked and stroked, she made a mental note of what made him curse or say her name, everything that made him lose a little control.

But she didn't want him to come the first time in her mouth. She had thought about being with him for too long not to want him deep inside her the first time. Pulling away from him, she moved back up his body with kisses. As she bit and nibbled at his lips, she reached into her nightstand for the condoms she had bought in preparation for their first date. She had hoped it would lead to here but hadn't pushed. Now she wished she'd had.

She sat up, still straddling him as she carefully opened the packet and rolled the condom on him. His eyes were on her the entire time, but he didn't make a move to help. He just watched her work.

With him still watching, she shifted again, her hand still around him as she aligned him to her. Slowly, she sank down onto him in one smooth motion. The heady sensations of her body stretching around him made her whisper his name in pleasure. She had missed this feeling.

Anderson's hands went to her thighs and squeezed as he shifted under her, making the sensations shoot right through her. Their bodies were completely still as his hands went from her thighs to her breasts, then squeezed them gently.

"You, okay?" he asked, his voice thick with need.

"Oh, so much better than okay," she said and started to rock, which took her breath away.

Taking it as the encouragement he needed, he started moving, thrusting up to meet her, sending sensations throughout her body.

With his hands back on her hips, she lifted slowly, feeling him tremble beneath her, loving that he was barely holding on.

Her confidence was building, and before she knew it, she was no longer in control. Her body knew what it wanted, and she was just along for the ride. As she rode him, his thumb massaged her clit, making quick, soft circles that sent her straight over the edge.

Her body was still pulsing and writhing when she felt his orgasm overtake him. Watching his pleasure made her spasm again.

After a while, Anderson rolled her onto her side and tucked her body into his as they tried to catch their breath. They were facing each other, and Anderson grabbed the edge of the comforter that was somewhat below them. It barely covered their naked bodies but was close enough. Ruth realized she wasn't moving to fix it.

Now cocooned under the blanket, Anderson ran a finger over her cheek. "Happy Valentine's Day, Ruth."

"Happy Valentine's Day, Anderson." She breathed him in as she said it, burrowing closer to him.

CHAPTER 15

ANDERSON WRAPPED his arms around Ruth from behind as she worked on cutting cheese. Since she had her white blonde hair in a braid that ran down her back, he was able to nibble on her neck as she worked. She elbowed him in the gut, laughing as she scolded him. "Leave me alone, Anderson. I need to get this tray together before the girls get here. I want them to think I am not completely lost in the kitchen."

"Except you are." He trailed kisses up to her ear and felt her shiver in his arms.

"But I don't want them to know that." She set the knife down and turned into his arms to meet his lips with her own. As she kissed him, he let her take the lead. He knew they wouldn't make it into the bedroom because the book club would arrive in a few minutes, but it didn't matter, as long as they were kissing. But still, he wanted to see how far she would go.

Not that he wouldn't happily take this to the bedroom again, even if they had made love twice already that morning.

The relief he had felt yesterday when he had finally found her in her kitchen had turned instantly to anger. There she was, after two days of not answering her phone or texts, just hiding. She had been standing innocently in her kitchen, eating a sandwich with cordless headphones on so loud he could hear the buzz of music from the doorway. Just in sweats and a T-shirt, she looked so defeated when she had seen him heartbroken. Instantly, he had watched her turn into personal assistant Ruth, cold and aloof. Distant.

Everything he had suspected she had concluded about Daphne's call had been exactly what she had been thinking. Why would she think that with just a phone call, he would leave her and go back to his ex? But he knew the answer to that. Franky had destroyed her when he left. The call made her think that Anderson was leaving her as well. He saw it in her eyes when he walked in the door that she had been hurting, thinking he was gone. That she had taken second place again.

For two days, he had thought she had given up on them, but he'd been frantic to find her and get her back. And she had been spent those days thinking he didn't want her anymore, that he would just leave her the moment someone else showed up. Just like her first love had.

That look was what made him panic when she talked about quitting. What would she do if she didn't work for him? What would he do if she didn't work for him? The office would turn into a dull and boring place.

She pushed him away, breathing heavily as she looked at him with those pale blue eyes. "Quit that," she said, like it hadn't been her that had started to kiss him.

The front door suddenly opened, interrupting their standoff. Both spun to look at the new arrivals.

Anderson watched as Tess from the bank and a short-haired blonde entered. Both were carrying a book, and they were chatting with each other as they came in. Neither seemed to notice that they were interrupting something.

Tess was the first to notice him, and she smiled. "You are joining us, Anderson?"

Beside him, Ruth tensed and said, "No, he is leaving."

"Too bad," the bank president said. "It would be nice to have a man's perspective."

Anderson didn't know the woman very well, but he knew of her, as did everyone in town. What he knew was that she had become one of Ruth's best friends in just a few short weeks. All these women had.

"I would be happy to stay and give my opinion. What book are you reading this week?" He watched both women walk to the kitchen area and dropped off the trays of food they were carrying.

Instead of answering right away, Tess sat on a barstool before asking with all seriousness, "Does tying up women turn you on?"

Anderson choked on the piece of cheese in his mouth and stared at the woman. *"What?"*

Ruth slapped him on the back as if he was choking, which he was. "Tess, leave him alone. The book this week is BTK. I assume her next question will be about torture."

"Of course, it was." Tess laughed and popped a piece of cheese into her mouth.

Anderson turned to Ruth, who was biting her bottom lip to control her laugh. Cupping her chin in his hand, he kissed the bottom lip that she was biting so cutely. "I will head out so you can enjoy book club."

As he walked out of the apartment, he heard Tess quietly say something about him, but he decided he didn't need to know what. Slipping on his shoes in the hallway, he saw the tall, dark-haired librarian, Natalie, making her way up the stairs with a bag over her shoulder and a box in her arms. Hurrying down the stairs, he grabbed the box from her, and she rewarded him with a smile.

"This is a lot of stuff for a book club," he said as the weight of the box was heavier than he had expected it to be.

"Have you ever been a part of a book club?" the younger woman asked with a raised eyebrow.

"No."

"Then you don't know what's involved," she stated as they walked into the apartment. The women present greeted the new arrival. He set the box by the door, not wanting to interfere in Ruth's girl time. After two days of not knowing where she was, he realized he liked to spend all his time with her. But she had friends.

Not bothering to say goodbyes again, he slipped out the door without a word. Ruth was joking with the women in the room. Her smile made him smile as he walked down the stairs.

He almost ran into Mia at Ruth's street-level door. The landing was small, and he and Mia did a little dance as they tried to get past each other. Mia was carrying two bottles of alcohol and a bottle of coke. Laughing when she finally got past him, she headed up the stairs but stopped on the first step.

"You finally found her?"

"Yes, yesterday," he replied, realizing he had forgotten to call her when he found Ruth as he had promised.

"Where was she? I never saw her mom come for her."

"She said she was here the entire time, but I checked every few hours, even in the middle of the night." Anderson still hadn't figured out where she had disappeared to.

So far, he hadn't asked her again where she had been. They had talked about other things, but that hadn't been a topic they had discussed. Mostly because he had forgotten, and he knew she wouldn't bring it up. After all, it was her secret.

"Ruth Kennedy has some secrets, and I have been trying to crack her for years. So many questions." She shifted the bottles in her arms.

"Like what?"

"Like why she's never left. After Franky left her, she had nothing to keep her here. I know he broke her heart, and she needed time to get over that, but she could have done that anywhere." Her pink head bobbed as she talked.

"She told me it was for her mom."

"I call bull. Her mom wasn't even twenty when she had Ruth, so that makes her around fifty today. Healthy as a horse, and she has Chester, so she doesn't need Ruth living right here. Something else."

"I guess we will have to wait until she tells us." Anderson was done pushing; Ruth was in charge now.

"You don't know her very well; she doesn't tell her secrets." Mia juggled the bottles in her arms for a moment again.

"What else do you want to know?" he asked.

"Where she gets her money. You don't pay that well, and neither did Frank Berg." She grinned at him.

"She doesn't have money," he said, though the comment stung. Was it a joke, or did people actually see him as cheap?

"No, she doesn't spend money, Anderson. She *has* it. You know that the table of hers was left by someone who had moved out of Tess's apartment a few years ago. I was eyeing it until she took it. Meanwhile, her sound system in there cost her a few grand," Mia said, shifting her bottles again.

He had noticed that expensive system the first night in the apartment, but since she used it so much, he saw she felt it was worth the money. Then he recognized that the headphones she was wearing yesterday were an expensive brand. But Mia was right; most of her furniture was old and worn.

He defended his lack of knowledge of her finances. "She has no car payment, and her car is a 70s-something that needs a new muffler."

"Do you not know cars? 1970 Dodge Charger in bright green? That car is probably worth fifty grand, Anderson. There's a reason she only drives it a few days a year, and every year, it is worth more and more." Mia finally turned and headed up the stairway.

Watching her go, he wondered about the car. He had only seen it a few times. Usually, it was parked outside the building, rarely driven around. And never in bad weather.

Once back out onto the street, he circled to the office and unlocked that door. Book club would only take a few hours, and he thought he could get some stuff done while she wasn't there to distract him.

After a few minutes, he realized that he missed her. He hadn't been in the office since after she had stormed out days before. Their lunches were still sitting on her desk. Getting up, he tossed them in her garbage can and looked at her desk. It was a little messy since she had left abruptly.

A bell dinged as the office door opened, and Rafferty swaggered in. "Did you ever find Angel then?"

Smiling at his friend, he said, "Yes, she was home all the time."

"That's Ruth. She's usually in this building. I would have told you to check the basement, but I know she is scared of spiders, so she wouldn't go down there." Rafferty pulled a chair in front of Ruth's desk and sat down. Anderson sat down in her chair.

"It's snakes, actually. How do you know there is a basement?"

"Franky used to dare everyone to go down there. It is spooky, and I am sure the water heater and furnace are down there."

"Did Frank Berg always have his office here?"

"Yup, bought the place and moved the Mrs in upstairs when they came to town before Franky was born. Then they bought the house on Fourth." Rafferty grabbed Ruth's candy jar and took out a piece.

"So, Frank owned it?" Anderson question.

"Yeah, he did. I wonder why he sold it to someone that wasn't taking over the insurance office?" Rafferty noisily opened the candy.

"I don't know. I know it wasn't an option. My dad would have bought it." He knew his dad almost didn't buy the branch when the building was not included. And for a few years, he had wanted to buy a building to move into, but every time he found a place, it was bought before he could even look at it.

"Did you make up with her?"

"Yes, and it pushed our relationship a bit further." He couldn't not smile at the memory of Ruth and the last twenty-four hours. An amazing twenty-four hours.

"No need for details. I don't want to know."

Rafferty, who was always willing to share the details of his love life, didn't want to hear Anderson's. He had asked about Daphne and his relationship, so it was only Anderson's relationship with Ruth that he didn't want to hear about.

"What do you know about Ruth's car?" Mia's words were running through his head.

"That she has a lot of money tied up in that car. It's gorgeous and a man's wet dream, but not really what I picture Ruth in." Rafferty took another candy.

"Why do you think she got it?"

"I remember it being Franky's dream car, but I sometimes wonder if it was hers, and she talked him into it being his. She bought it about five years after the transplant, so maybe it was just a gift for surviving."

For a moment, he just stared at the man across from him. "I didn't think a lot of people knew about the transplant. She said nobody in town knew."

Shrugging, Rafferty said, "I am one of the few. I don't tell people her secrets."

"Why did her mom let her move in with Franky at sixteen?" If anyone knew, it was Rafferty. They had run in the same circles back then.

"Because Chester was very abusive to Angel. He was drinking pretty heavy then and didn't like sassy teenagers. Frank actually told Sara that if she wanted her kid back, she had to leave Chester. Sara stayed, so Ruth stayed with Frank and Lynn until she graduated and never moved back in with her mom. Frank always had a soft spot for her. He took her side in the breakup and didn't invite Franky to work with him when the guy graduated, even when it meant that he had nobody to take over for him, and he had to sell. The office was Ruth's space, not Franky's." Rafferty took another candy from the jar.

"How abusive?" Anderson demanded. Ruth had never hinted at that.

"I don't know the true extent of it, just rumors from back then. But a lot of hitting and yelling. Usually, Angel would leave and come into town when it started. Always staying with Franky's family." He cringed at the word.

"She goes out there every weekend." Until this moment, he had never had any worries about her going out to her mom's. But now he might have to talk to her about it. If there was abuse out there, Ruth shouldn't be going.

"I think once she was an adult, he stopped trying to control her. And he doesn't drink like he used to, either." Rafferty put the candy jar down.

"I can't see her putting up with that now," Anderson agreed.

"You're going to have to meet the dragon lady if you're going to keep seeing Ruth. She is going to hate you." Rafferty laughed.

"You mean her mother. Yes, I hope I can meet her one day and see where Ruth came from." He had hoped to have met her by now, but Ruth never brought it up.

"She is going to hate you," Rafferty repeated. His laughter stopped, and his face was serious.

"Why? What have I done?" he asked.

"You are having sex with her baby with no ring on her finger. But then again, it might also just be that you are a man who is interested in her baby." Rafferty looked out the window at the snowy street. "Either way, you better be sure that you are in for the long haul if you meet her."

Anderson was silent as he thought about what Rafferty was saying. He enjoyed spending time with Ruth, but was he looking at forever with her? He had once thought that Daphne was the one, and that had only been a few months ago after so many years. But Ruth was different from Daphne. Ruth was not a career woman and would probably follow him anywhere. He knew that he didn't want to stay in Landstad forever, and he was starting to think that he wanted to take Ruth with him when he left.

With so much on his mind, he decided it was time to go home. Maybe he'd pack some stuff so that he could stay with Ruth another night. All he had to do was wait for her text saying that the girls had left.

After saying goodbye to Rafferty in the cold, in front of the office, he glanced up at her window. The lights were blazing inside as he got into his truck and drove home.

Ruth had a lot of layers that needed to be peeled back. How many? Anderson couldn't say yet, but he was excited to find out about them all.

CHAPTER 16

WAKING SUDDENLY, Ruth wondered what had snapped her from sleep? Without moving, she listened to the sounds in her mostly quiet apartment. There was nothing but Anderson's breathing behind her. She was tucked against him, and he had an arm over her body, holding her close to him.

Then she heard the faint beeping again. Sighing, she knew what the sound was, but now she would have to fix it before she could sleep again and had to shut it off before it woke Anderson up. Her body didn't want to leave Anderson, but her mind demanded she go fix the error.

Slowly and carefully, she pulled out from under his arm. When she was free, she looked down at him sleeping there in her bed and loved the sight. She wanted to touch him but didn't. She would be right back.

They had been sleeping together for almost three weeks. He had practically been living with her the entire time. They spent all day working together and all evening chatting and eating together, then the nights were filled with touching and making love. Ruth had never been so happy. Though she hadn't been able to write all that much, she was willing to sacrifice that for spending time with Anderson.

Grabbing her bathrobe off the back of the door, she slipped through the apartment and across the hall into her writing office. The beeping was far louder in here, and the lights were blinking red. In the near dark, she pushed a few buttons, which made the annoying beeping go silent. Once it was quiet, she turned a nob down, then back up and hit a few more buttons. Then she moved to the computer and nudged it back on, typed in her password, and went to the program she was looking for.

Finally, she sat in her chair and started to save the programs she had opened, then shut down that computer. Turning around, she closed down the computer that sat behind her, the one that ran the large network system sitting above it. After the computer shut down and it was black in the room, she turned that computer back on. She watched it run through the startup process, making sure everything was going right. *Maybe it's time to replace some network equipment*, she thought. She typed in a few keys when the right screen popped up, and the whirling and beeping behind her said the system was back online. Moving back to the main computer, she turned it on and watched the screen as the computer came to life.

"What is this?" The words from the dark room made her jump.

Breathing heavily and looking around in the darkness beyond her screen in front of her, she didn't see him. But he was there, so she innocently explained. "This is your computer network, Anderson. It went down, and I had to reboot it. Did I wake you?"

"I don't know whether to believe you or not. Is this where you were on Valentine's Day?" His voice was still coming from the darkness beyond.

Reaching under her desk, she turned on the light switch she had under there. Every corner in the little apartment sudden was lit. Anderson was standing near the door, looking sexy in his underwear. Angry and sexy.

"Yes, I needed to get away," she admitted.

"At least now I know where to find you next time. What is all this stuff?"

"This, Anderson, is your computer network. It has been

supporting your work for five years. And three before that." She watched his eyes take in the wall of equipment behind her.

Suddenly, she was embarrassed by the surrounding room. She had never expected anyone to come in here. Though the wall of equipment, computer desk, and computer were newer, the rest of the place was run-down and shabby. The orange carpet had seen better days, and there was paneling on the walls. The couch had a sheet over it, but it looked lumpy and old. She occasionally slept on it when she was working late into the night…or when she was avoiding people who might come into her apartment looking for her, like on Valentine's Day.

"I am not going to lie, this is weird. I don't think we need this much equipment for the office. We only have two computers. This is a major amount of networking equipment." He walked towards it and looked closer at it. She wondered if he actually knew that.

"You have two printers down stairs also. And all this stuff is already paid for. So no going back now," she said. She had bought the equipment when she started to run the websites for her author pages. Since she wrote books under five names, she maintained five websites. She knew how to keep them up, so she hadn't had to pay anything for the systems for years. Frank had been okay with her putting his equipment on the system. He didn't even ask her why she needed the equipment.

He turned to her in question. "How do you know how to fix it?"

"I read the manual when I got it," she explained, and it was the truth. Computers were not her interest, but it had been a surprisingly straightforward system.

"Is this the computer you have to use to fix it?" He touched the top of one of her monitors.

"Sometimes, but most of the system stuff is on that one." She pointed at an identical one behind her, below the network equipment. When she had upgraded to a new computer the year prior, she had just bought the same kind but a newer model.

"Do you know a lot about computer networking?" He gestured to her wall of equipment.

"No, but I know how to keep up with this one." Again, it was the truth, and she truly dreaded updating her system.

"Do I pay you to keep this up?" He pointed at it all again. Now that the fans were spinning, it was getting louder in the room.

"No."

"I should be." He crossed his arms.

"No, Anderson, I…" She had no idea how to say what she was thinking. In reality, she still didn't want to.

"What?" His confusion was turning back into anger.

"I do things for you to make up for what I do," she tried to explain but knew she wasn't doing that great of a job.

"Now say that in English, Ruth." He put his hands on his hips.

"I run the network since I bought the network and installed it. I also pay for the internet in the building, as well as the heating and cooling in the building." She ran her fingers through her hair.

"Those are included in rent, Ruth," he replied. That was what was in his rental contract.

"No, I pay them. Rent is separate and would be higher if I didn't take advantage of you like I do." She bit her lip, waiting for his anger. She deserved it.

"What exactly do you do?" He eyed her skeptically

"I, um, do very little work at the office. I do everything you ask, I swear, but I have a lot of free time." She lowered her head and stared at the orange carpet.

"You are constantly working. You are typing or reading all the time. I don't even know how you keep so busy." He squatted down in front of her and took her hands. Concerned about her reaction.

"But I don't do that for you. I do it for me. I write books for a living, and I just work for you to keep busy," she admitted and held her breath. She had only said those words a few times in her life. She never told anyone about her actual job. Even her mom was in the dark about how she made money.

"So, you write books at work?" he asked in confusion.

"Rarely. I usually edit them there. I write here."

"What kind of books?"

"Romance novels." She peeked up at him, wishing she could say suspense or mystery. Even owner's manuals would be less embarrassing than admitting to writing sexy, smutty books. But there is nothing else she would want to write.

"I want to say you are pulling my leg about this." He ran his thumb over her cheek, thinking she was kidding him.

Getting up, she pulled him to a shelf on the wall that had been there for years. On it was close to ninety books. "These are mine. I get a copy of each one that is published."

He scanned the shelf. "None of these have your name on them, Ruth."

She had them grouped by author name. He was right; none of them were under Mary or Ruth or Johnson or Kennedy. She had picked unique names for each of her pen names.

"I write under different names."

"How many do you do a year?" He pulled one out and looked at the cover. It was a scantily clad couple in an embrace. The guy was shirtless, and the woman was close to it.

"Around eight now." She was proud of her accomplishment.

"When did you start?" He put the book back in its place.

"The first fall when I was working for Frank, and Franky was at school. Frank usually took an afternoon nap, and I was really bored. I started writing letters to Franky, but he complained that it was too much reading. So, then I started writing short stories. It was quiet, and I could do it in the office. Then I started reading romance novels in the evenings since I was alone. One day, I decided I should try to write one. I finished it just before my transplant. Afterwards, I sent it to an editor, and they published it. I just kept going. Frank didn't care what I did."

She bit her lip. "But I felt bad working on my stuff when you came. I tried to stop, but I had nothing to do all day. I just edit now. But I give you perks, like internet and computer stuff. Do you hate me?"

He leaned against the wall. "When you are sitting at your desk blushing, what are you editing?"

"Sex scenes. They always make me blush in the office. I sometimes think you can hear what I am reading."

"The day of the bonfire before Mia came in, were you editing a sex scene?" he demanded.

"Yes. Could you tell?" She had finished the book about Jessa and Link, and it was one of her favorites, maybe simply because of that scene.

Cupping her chin in his hands, he brushed a thumb across her lips. "I think I could. I wanted to have sex with you right there on your desk."

"The scene took place on your desk," she whispered.

He pulled her close to him. "I will never look at that desk the same again."

"I have written sex scenes everywhere in that office. Recently, I have written a lot of office romances." She felt herself blush.

"I am going to have sex with you in this room, right now." He opened her robe to reveal she was naked beneath it, making him grin.

"I have a desk over there." She let the robe fall from her shoulders.

He pulled her to him, then turned her around and pinned her against the wall. "Too far away."

A shiver of excitement ran through her as his mouth claimed hers. Ruth was glad he knew her secret, or one of them at least. There was time for the others later. She was busy now.

CHAPTER 17

ANDERSON WATCHED Ruth's fingers fly across the keyboard, wondering how fast she actually could type. Then he wondered what she was writing. It had been a week since she had told him that she was a writer.

That night he hadn't really believed her; he was too turned on by her crazy computer skills. Who would have thought? But then again, they had never had any computer issues. Not ever. He remembered once having an error pop up before the end of the day a few years before. By morning the computer was fine—had she fixed it for him?

Then she had taken it into overdrive by admitting she read or wrote sex scenes from her desk a few feet from him while he was there. All he could think about was the sexual tension that was swirling around them the day of the bonfire, and this time he could act on it. And he did.

In the month since they had turned their relationship sexual, she had changed for the better again. In the bedroom, she was bold and adventurous, and it turned him on. He couldn't get enough of her. During the day, he could barely keep his hands off her and had taken to touching her when he could. Just a quick caress now and again. She had responded by doing the same.

Oddly, he hadn't told Mia or Rafferty what he had found out, mainly because Ruth didn't want people to know. So far, he hadn't pushed to see if there were more secrets. Maybe he didn't want to know.

"Stop watching me, Anderson. Go get lunch if you are bored." She was looking at him over her glasses.

Jumping up, he strode across the room and kissed her. But before it could go too far, he headed out the door to the café. Once there, he took a seat on a stool and placed his order with a waitress. It looked like Mia was off today. She usually joked with him or had a few juicy pieces of gossip to tell.

When the boxes were set in front of him, it reminded him of the lunches that went uneaten on Valentine's Day. He grinned, glad he knew where to find her the next time she disappeared.

Pushing through the door, he called out to her, "Open face sandwich today, your favorite."

The words died on his lips when he saw his brother leaning against Ruth's desk, looking down at her. His posture said that he was interested in the personal assistant and was trying to look down her blouse. Anger rushed through Anderson at the sight.

"Andy, you came back. Ruthie here said you went for lunch but would be back quickly." His brother turned to him and away from Ruth as if he hadn't been staring at her moments before.

"Jonathan," he said in a way of greeting.

"Anything good?" He took the boxes from Anderson's hand.

"Get your own lunch," Anderson stated.

"Ham sandwich. I will take that one. I love those." Jonathan gave the other box to Anderson and went into his office, then sat in Anderson's chair and opened the box.

Ruth gave him a weary look as Anderson followed his brother into the other office. He could tell that Jonathan had been there long enough for Ruth. She had no tolerance for some people, and it seemed his brother had easily made that list.

Anderson sat down in one of the guest chairs across from his own chair. His brother had long made that list for Anderson.

"Mom hasn't seen you in months," Jonathan scolded him.

"I have talked to her, and she knows I like to stay here as much as possible." It was the truth. Another truth was that he hated leaving Ruth. He hated being away from her but hadn't known if he was ready for her to meet his family. Except now, she was in the worst possible way.

"She says you met someone." Jonathan ate a chip with a grin. "Nobody like Daphne, though. She was hot. And she was good in bed. But I don't have to tell you that, do I?"

"Can we not talk about that? I am over her," he hissed, wishing that Ruth wasn't so close. Not that he even thought about the woman anymore, not with Ruth in his life.

"What? Only your secretary can hear us. And she is probably interested in knowing that kind of information, office gossip and all." Jonathan pointed at Ruth with a chip.

Every time Jonathan called her a secretary, Anderson cringed. The word from Jonathan's mouth made it seem like he was belittling those beneath him. It was a term that turned his stomach and had for years.

"She is my personal assistant." He shot Ruth a look as she stared at her computer, but her fingers were not moving, so she was listening.

"Wait, is she your rebound?" Jonathan sat up straighter, his own eyes swinging toward the blonde.

"We are not talking about this," Anderson stated firmly.

"So, it is her. You are having sex with your secretary? She is hot, though." He grinned and took a bite of the stolen sandwich as he looked over at Ruth.

"Jonathan," he warned, tired of his brother being there.

"They are always ready for a man when they get done with you, Andy." He finished the sandwich with a smirk and rubbed the crumbs off his hands.

Ruth walked into the room with two cups in her hands. "Coffee."

Anderson had started to recognize her moods. This one was her prickly secretary. This was the Ruth he'd known during the first four years they knew each other.

"Sure, sweetheart. Andy says that you are sleeping together." Jonathan tossed the empty food container on the desk.

"I don't believe that is what he said," Ruth said emotionlessly, setting both cups on the desk.

"You're pretty hot, Ruthie," he replied with a wink.

"And you are sexually harassing me, Mr. Miles." Still cool, collected Ruth.

"I am not, just paying you a compliment," Jonathan insisted smoothly.

"You want to sleep with me?" she asked, leaning against the door-jamb. Anderson did not know what she was doing.

"If Andy doesn't mind, I am willing. Heck, even if he does mind, I am willing." Jonathan sat up straighter.

"You think I would just move from his bed to yours? Why would you even think that?" Her arms were folded as she looked down at Jonathan, who was still in Anderson's chair.

"I am a lot better than he is in bed, if you are interested, Ruthie." He smirked again and leaned back in the chair, relaxing into the conversation.

Anderson watched Ruth looking at his brother. Was she comparing the two? Was she trying to come up with a comeback? Her blue eyes held a hint of anger in them, and her nose was flared with annoyance.

"Are you asking me to have sex with you? In the office?" She looked around the room, avoiding Anderson's eyes as she did.

"I would have sex with you in the office." His brother was not seeing the annoyance in her eyes.

"Mr. Miles, what you are doing is called sexual harassment." She pointed out.

"You started it," he whined.

"So, I am to blame for your wrongdoing? Me, a secretary from Landstad, made you do it?" Ruth stated, taking a step towards Jonathan. "Or was it you and your self-importance? Because I wasn't the one who slept with your brother's girlfriend. I am not the one who cheated on your wife, and I am not the one who spent five minutes looking down my shirt. That, Jonathan, was all you."

"I don't need a lecture from you." He was finally catching on and stood up from the chair, taking a step away from Ruth.

"You need it from someone. Go back to your wife, Jonathan. She deserves better, but she has you. I have no interest in you. And if you say one more word to me, other than about insurance, I will report you to your father. I have his number, and as an employee, I can make your career die." She took a step towards him, causing him to take one back. For the first time in his life, Jonathan looked scared.

"Y-you wouldn't," Jonathan stammered.

"Don't tempt me. I have nothing to lose. I get job offers all the time, and not one is from my daddy. So, I could get another job within ten minutes of stepping out that door. Can you say the same thing?" Ruth turned and walked back to her desk.

Jonathan watched her and stood up. "I have to go." He then hurried out of the office without saying another word.

After the door slammed shut, Anderson got up and walked to her desk. She was staring out the window, watching Jonathan get in his car, not working. "What was that?"

"Sorry, I just had to tell him off for what he has done to you." Ruth turned back to him.

"You are amazing. You chased him out of here!" He pulled her out of her chair and kissed her on the lips in front of the big window, not caring if his brother looked back to see them, or anyone else for that matter.

"It was sexual harassment," she insisted.

"Was that kiss sexual harassment?" he questioned.

She smirked. "The kiss was not unwanted."

"Have you ever had a job offer before?"

"Yes, every few months. The school around Christmas and Dale Riley last week. I am seen around town as a great personal assistant who's poorly paid." She bit her lip. That meant it was true;, because if it wasn't she would have denied it.

"Why do you stay? What keeps you working for me when you

could leave at any moment?" He looked into her pale blue eyes, just now realizing how close he had come to losing her before he had gotten to know her.

"I told you, I enjoy working here. I don't need the money." She held his gaze.

"I guess I still have a hard time believing you make enough money for anything with your books." He let her go and walked back to his desk.

"I do okay." He watched her sit down and reach for her lunch. "Do you want to share?"

What he wanted was to close the office and drag her upstairs and make love to her. Or maybe just pull her into his office and shut the door. But he would be a professional and let her eat her lunch. Then he would suggest they close for lunch and have a quickie.

CHAPTER 18

THE SUN WAS RISING in the east, and it promised to be a warm day—if twenty degrees was warm. In Landstad, in March, it was. It was Monday morning, and since last night had been book club, he had slept at his house for the first time in well over a month. He missed waking up with Ruth, and he missed going to sleep with her also.

It had been a week since his brother had come for a visit. Since then, Anderson had not heard from his father or Jonathan, and his mother had not mentioned anything about it, which meant that his brother didn't share much about his trip to Landstad with them if anything. Ruth must have really gotten to his brother.

Ruth had not spent the weekend with her mother in a few weeks. Her mother picked her up Saturday before lunch and dropped her off just before supper that same day, but she was not staying out there. So far, Anderson had not been invited out. Ruth didn't suggest an introduction, and he didn't push.

Anderson parked in the free parking area a block from the office. He had gotten used to parking there, so he didn't have to move his truck when the snowplows wanted to go through in the middle of the night. As he walked, he saw Ruth's door swing open. Was she getting to work early? Did she miss him?

But instead of Ruth walking out the door, he watched as Rafferty Brooks rushed out of the door and headed away from him. The man was practically running down the sidewalk when he plowed into Mia coming out of the post office. Ignoring both of them, he jogged to Ruth's door, pulling it open and rushing up the stairs.

He couldn't believe it. The moment he was gone, she had Rafferty up here. Had he been there all night? Were they having an affair? He had point-blank asked both of them about each other, and both had been adamant that nothing had ever happened. But he knew there was something between them; he could feel it.

Why had he trusted her? Just because she didn't want to sleep with his brother didn't mean she wouldn't sleep with someone else. Rafferty. Anderson's friend…or former friend now.

No time to take off his shoes or jacket—it wouldn't take long to tell her off. He was tired of women who slept around. After Daphne, he should have noticed the signs earlier except he still didn't notice than.

Opening the door without knocking, he expected her to be in the shower, cleaning up and getting ready for the day. Getting ready for a day in the office with him after sleeping with Rafferty.

Instead, she was sitting on the couch, staring out the window at the rising sun. She was wearing a skirt and blouse and had her hair up, ready for the day. Over her shoulder, he saw her pull out her phone and type something out, then drop the phone, which fell to the floor with a thud. His phone in his pocket indicated that he had a text. Lifting it up, he read:

Ruth: I am taking a sick day.

It was from Ruth. Ruth, in front of him. She turned at the sound his phone had made. Her eyes were filled with unshed tears, but she said nothing, just turned away from him.

"What is wrong? What did Rafferty do?" He went around the couch, pulling off his coat and dropping it on the floor before sitting down next to her.

"He was nice to me." She turned back to the window.

"Did he hurt you?" Pulling her into his arms, he held her to him. Something in her tone had him on edge. He had always liked Rafferty, but that would change if he had done something to Ruth. She went into his arms willingly.

"No, never. But I have hurt him. Again and again over the years."

"Ruth?" He had no idea what to say. What was happening?

"Did you know that when we were six in the school Christmas program, he was a shepherd, and I was an angel. I was always the stupid angel. He was the only one who saw that the binding that was holding me up in the air was breaking. He tried to catch me. We both broke our arms. My left, and his right." She looked at the arm that had once been broken.

"You never told me that."

"When we were eight, and Kyle Kenny stole by bike, Rafferty got it back for me." Her voice cracked a little. "I didn't even have to ask him to; he just did it. I think he was grounded for fighting with him over my bike."

"Sounds like a nice kid." He wondered what made her think of all these things.

"When I was sick half the year when we were ten, he brought me my homework every day. He said it was because he had to walk by my place anyway." She leaned into him even more.

All he did was shake his head, knowing she didn't want an answer. She just wanted to talk.

"When we were thirteen, we were at a party, and we played seven minutes in heaven. I spun the bottle, and it landed on Rafferty. I was already dating Franky. We went into the closet and just talked. He didn't try to kiss me or touch me. We sat in the back of the closet, just talking about stuff. Then at the very end, he bumped his shoulder to my shoulder and said I was his favorite girlfriend, a girl who was a friend." The tears were now flowing.

"He is a nice guy." Anderson had seen that side of Rafferty and thought that Ruth hadn't, but it seemed that she had seen it over the years. He wondered why she had mostly ignored it.

"Too nice to me. I have been so mean to him. He came over and told me Howard died. He could have called or just let me find out through the gossip of town. But he took the time to stop by, and I was the first person he told. After everything I have said and done to him in the last few years, he still came," she said.

"His dad died?" he asked. He hadn't heard that.

She didn't answer, just fell silent as she looked out the bright window, letting the tears fall from her eyes. She didn't even wipe them away. It bothered him how she was affected by what was happening in the Brooks family.

"Howard always wanted me dead." She wiped her tears, but more came quickly. "He waited eighteen years for my kidneys to fail. Everybody knew that they would; it was just a matter of time. Maybe that's why I hung on to Franky all through school. I planned to marry him and have kids, but deep down, I didn't believe I would live that long. Then the minute Rafferty knew he could maybe help, he did."

"Mom asked Howard to be checked to see if we would be a match —if he could give me the kidney I needed. He said no. For nine years, he said no. She asked Rafferty, and he said yes and got tested that day. Within a week, I got the transplant. He saved my life, and I never even thanked him for doing it." She cried in his arms.

"Why was Rafferty able to give you his kidney?" Anderson wasn't following her logic.

"Howard was my dad, too. Rafferty is my half-brother," she whispered.

At her words, so many conversations and actions of Rafferty fell into place. Why he would never be interested in Ruth but knew so much about her. His reaction when she almost passed out at the bar. She had been sick most of her life, and something could happen again. He had actually said they were related at the café that morning so many months ago. Anderson had forgotten that.

"Don't be mad that I never told you. I have never told anyone, ever. Mom didn't tell me until I was in the hospital, dying."

"How?" he asked in confusion. Ruth and Rafferty were in the same grade in school. Wasn't Howard married when they were born?

"They had a fifteen-year affair, and it ended when she decided she wanted better and married Chester. She has bad taste in men. I happened within the first few years, but he never acknowledged me, ever. I was thirteen when they broke it off. Rafferty got the dad I always wanted, but I don't think he got a good dad. I was so angry with Howard for rejecting me that I punished Rafferty for it. I am a bad person. For all these years, I have been a bad person." She buried her head in his suit jacket and cried.

"Ruth." He just held her in his arms. Let her cry tears for the man who would never be her dad.

As her tears dried up, she sat up. "I need to go see my mom and tell her. I don't want her to find out from gossip."

"Do you want me to go, or do you just want to use my pickup?" he asked, not wanting to push her into meeting her mom and stepdad. At this point, he wanted to meet them, but was she also feeling they were ready to meet each other's parents already?

She surprised him with her answer. "Can you come?"

Ruth changed out of her business attire and washed her face to get ready to see her mother. When she was done, she was wearing gray slacks and a blue sweater, and she had left her hair loose. He could tell the tears were near the surface, but she had them under control at that moment.

Winter was still in full swing, and the snow covered everything with inches to feet of the white fluffy stuff. Ruth directed him to her mother's place. It seemed to take longer than Anderson had expected, but soon they were pulling in front of a small ranch house nestled among gray outbuildings. In the cover of winter, it was quaint and picturesque.

Ruth barely waited for the pickup to stop before she jumped out and headed for the door. Anderson was unable to catch up to her before she made it there. By the time Anderson made it into the house, Ruth was in the kitchen. The house was small, and Anderson made it into the room as Ruth's mom turned from the sink and leaned against the counter with her hands on her chest.

Her mother was not what he had ever expected. From what Mia had said, she was barely a day over fifty, but her life had been harder than her daughter's, and it showed in her face. Despite that, she was just an older version of Ruth. Same hair, same height, but Sara's eyes were brown, not Ruth's ice-blue.

"Angel, what are you doing here?" the older woman asked her daughter.

"Mom, I have something to tell you. Can you sit?" Ruth pulled out a chair for the woman.

"Who is this?" Sara Kennedy pointed at Anderson.

"Mom, can you sit? This is Anderson Miles," Ruth said with a wave in his direction.

"Your boss? What is he doing here?" Sara's back stiffened.

"He drove me here," Ruth tried to explain and tapped the chair again.

"I could have come and got you," Sara protested, looking at Anderson from head to toe. Her face said that she didn't like what she saw.

"I wanted to come out here and talk to you." Ruth finally gave up on the chair.

She pointed at Anderson again. "About him?"

"No, something else." Ruth walked to the stove. It was turned off, so Ruth just leaned on it, wrapping her fingers around the handle behind her.

"Should he be here, then?" Sara still had her eyes on Anderson. It didn't seem like she was going to get used to him being there.

"Yes, he knows what I am going to tell you. Can you sit down?" Ruth gestured to the chair.

"I can stand." She protested her daughter's request again.

"Please, Mom."

"No, I can stand."

"Howard is dead, Mom." Ruth's hands were wrapped around the stove handle, and her knuckles were white as she said the words.

"Good riddance," Sara spat out. Anderson could tell it was not the reaction Ruth was expecting by the shock in her face.

"Mom," Ruth said in way of warning.

"Okay, fine. But I have cried too many tears over that man. I have been done with him for years now." Sara turned and started to run water to rinse the cup she had been washing.

"I just wanted you to know." Ruth didn't move, her voice a little shaky.

"Who told you?" Sara watched the water run.

"Rafferty stopped by."

"Of course, he did." She was still watching the water, but Anderson could hear the bitterness in her voice. Without turning, she asked, "Has he told her yet?"

"His mother? I assume he has. They were still married." Ruth let go of the handle and flexed her fingers.

"You can leave; you told me." Sara shut off the water, dismissing her daughter, still not turning around.

"If you're sure? I can stay." Ruth walked over to the table and pushed in the chair she had taken out.

"No, you go. We will talk about him later." Sara finally turned around and was trying to ignore Anderson altogether.

"Him as in Anderson?" Ruth pushed. He didn't know what she wanted her mom to say.

"Your boss," Sara emphasized.

"He's more than that, Mom. We can talk about it later." Ruth walked over to her mom at the sink.

As he watched, her mom pulled her into a hug for the first time since they had been there. The older woman was holding her daughter tight, but neither of them was crying. Sara was whispering into her daughter's ear. He was unable to see Ruth's face as they had a short conversation that he couldn't hear.

Ruth pushed herself out of her mother's embrace, saying, "No, mom. Just no."

"Angel," Sara protested.

"No, Mom. We have to go." Ruth turned and walked away.

"Will I see you anymore?" He heard the pain in Sara's voice, as if Ruth had to choose between them.

"Yes, Mother. I will come on a weekend."

"To stay?" Sara demanded.

"No, I live only a short drive away. I don't need to stay."

"So, it's him over me?" Sara didn't look his way.

Ruth shocked Anderson with her answer. "Yes, Mom."

"He'll leave you too, Ruth,"

"I know, Mom. But for now, I get to be with him." A chill ran down Anderson's spine. Is that how she saw them? As temporary?

"He is just going to hurt you." Sara wasn't mincing words. Anderson understood why everyone called her the dragon. What came from her mouth was as dangerous as fire and hurt a lot more. She made it sound like he was going to hurt Ruth, and that was the last thing he wanted to do.

"I know, Mom. I hope you will be there for me when it happens," Ruth said, as if he hadn't heard what she had said, that he was going to hurt her.

Sara looked at her daughter and hesitated a moment as the two stared into each other's eyes. "I am always here for you. Just call."

"I will," Ruth replied but didn't make a move to her mother. She just turned and left the house.

Anderson followed behind, saying nothing, doing nothing. She was in such a hurry that she was in the truck before he could even get to the vehicle. Walking through the cold to get in his truck, he looked around at the small farm, trying to see a younger Ruth growing up here. A shiver ran through him at the thought that Ruth had left this tranquil farm to live with her boyfriend due to abuse.

Driving back to town, Ruth was silent. Was she thinking about the conversation she had with her mom, or was she thinking about her father being dead? Ruth's voice, stating firmly that he would leave her, was playing over and over in his mind.

"Do you really think I will leave you, Ruth?" He had to know.

Ruth was looking out the passenger window and didn't turn to him when she said, "Yes, you want to go back to Grand Forks. I will always stay here. This will come to an end."

"Why?" he demanded.

"Why what?" She turned to him. He thought that she would have tears in her eyes, but they were dry.

"Why are you staying here?"

"This is my town. I have never wanted to leave. It's the reason I was okay with Franky going to college without me. I wanted to be here. I am comfortable here." She waved her arm at the surrounding landscape.

"But you barely spend any time in the actual town."

"I know, but I also know that when I do, everyone will be friendly, and I can talk to any of them about anything or nothing." He looked at her, and she was smiling a little bit.

"I like that when Coach Miller comes in with a few players, that means volleyball season is starting, and they are looking for money for uniforms. I always donate, even if the uniform is almost the same as the last ones that they bought. Or when a small group come in around now from the high school and are looking for money for prom, I give a little and know that for another night, these kids will get a memory that they will take with them when they leave here. And I like when the town starts decorating for Christmas, and everyone does their part. Oh, and I love when the summer carnival happens."

"But you don't really take part in any of it," he reminded her.

"I live downtown, so I can be a part of it even if I don't go down there. I guess I have stopped being involved over the years. That's why I like to work for you. I can be in the action of downtown and watch the city through my window. I can talk to the people who stop by." She turned to look out the window again as the town came into view.

"And you stay for that? Have you ever thought about leaving?" he asked, because nothing he heard seemed like a good enough reason to stay there.

"No, not really. Nothing is really holding me here, but there are strings that keep me here. I've never tried to break those," she admitted when he pulled in front of the office. Before he could respond, she was out of the pickup and into her building.

Anderson took a moment to look around her world. Two blocks of buildings, most were nearly a hundred years old. Oddly, most were occupied—both business and upstairs apartments seemed to be full at all times. Only Rafferty's building had issues with both.

Anderson watched a man rush out of the post office into the bitter cold day. Though he was tightly bundled into his jacket, hat, and mittens, he knew the man. Was it comforting to Anderson to know that he knew this man? That's what Ruth liked about this town; that she knew everyone and what they were up to. Anderson realized he didn't care about that at all, and he didn't think he ever would.

Slowly, he got out of the truck and followed the path Ruth had taken into her building. After kicking off his shoes at the top of the stairs, he walked inside, but she wasn't in the main rooms. A moment later, he found her in bed, still fully dressed. He said down next to her.

"Go to work, Anderson. I just need a few minutes."

He knew she needed more than a few minutes. Maybe even days was too short of a time to get over losing a father that had never really a father at all.

"Okay, call me if you need me." He got up and pulled the blanket off the end of the bed and laid it over her. He watched as she pulled it closer around her, and he leaned down and kissed her forehead.

As he left the apartment, he wondered if he should just stay, but he felt that she just needed to be alone with her thoughts. Alone to sort out what Howard's passing meant to her.

Walking down to his office, he wondered what it meant for them. Was there even a future for them? Ruth was sure that there was not. The fact that she felt so confident about it ending meant that he was starting to think it also. Her doubts were becoming his doubts.

CHAPTER 19

THURSDAY TURNED out to be another sunny, warm day. Landstad was buzzing outside the window to the office. Ruth was watching people walking up and down the sidewalk with open jackets and no hats, and sometimes someone went by without a jacket altogether. North Dakota was having a heatwave, Ruth decided, as another non-jacket-wearer scurried by, pretending not to be cold in the breeze.

Howard's funeral was in ten minutes, just down the road. It was taking place in the same church she attended every week. Part of her wanted to go, to see who came, and to see if anyone noticed that she was there. But she stayed away, not wanting to intrude on his death. He'd never wanted her there.

Anderson had left fifteen minutes before, but before he left, he'd asked if she was sure she didn't want to go. Again, she said no, just like every other time he asked. After taking two days off, she had returned to work and had been okay. How long can you mourn someone who had spent years watching you die and never tried to help? After lying in bed all day Monday, she had spent Tuesday writing, being in her happy place.

Though she loved her relationship with Anderson and loved spending every moment she could with him, she was missing writing.

Gone were the weekends where she could just write and forget about everything else. Evenings where she would be up until the wee hours of the morning were also gone. Now she let those ideas float away as she lay in his arms, content.

At this point, she was nearly done editing everything she'd written. Even some of the stories that she'd written only a few thousand words then stopped working on have been edited. But she hadn't come up with anything new until the Tuesday after Valentine's Day. She didn't want to write at the office; she liked music and no distractions when she was working on her stories.

As she wondered how she was going to spend the next few hours at the office, not thinking about the funeral, Mia walked in. Grabbing a chair from the waiting area, she pulled it to the desk and sat down across from Ruth.

"Sorry about Howard. Rafferty told me. I hope you don't mind. I won't tell anyone," Mia said and leaned back in her chair.

"Thank you, Mia. I don't think about it much," Ruth lied.

"I am really surprised. I had no idea. I pride myself in being the pulse of this town." Mia smiled.

"You are, but we all have secrets."

"And I spend my days finding those out. Why do you think I am a waitress? Do you have any more?" Mia picked up a pen and started to click it over and over again.

"What all do you know about me?" Ruth leaned back in her chair and raised an eyebrow.

"Let's see, Mary Ruth Johnson Kennedy owns a number of buildings in this town and still wastes her time as a personal assistant for Anderson. But then again, she is sleeping with him." Mia smirked. "She has a brother from another mother and has his kidney, but he secretly hopes to get part of her liver one day when he destroys his."

Ruth laughed at Mia's description of Rafferty. She was starting to think Mia had it as bad for Rafferty as Rafferty had it for Mia, but both were too stubborn to admit it. She hoped that Mia would find someone else—Rafferty wasn't what her friend needed in her life.

"I think you have me all figured out, Mia," She replied, hoping to keep the rest of her secrets to herself.

"I am not going to lie, the Rafferty one floored me. You two are the same age, like the *same* age." Mia leaned towards her as if it were a secret.

"Yes, our birthdays are a week apart," Ruth confirmed.

Mia was silent as she thought about the news, though it was something she probably already knew. She scrunched up her nose. "That's gross."

"It is. Let's talk about something else," Ruth suggested.

Mia nodded. "Do you think Anderson would agree to be in the auction this year? I am in charge this time."

Every year the town had an auction to raise money for flood repairs. The town was close enough to the Red River that it flooded when spring hit, and there would inevitably be some damage. Over the years, it had become a tradition to have the auction before the flood happened so that they had the money ready for who needed it, right when it was needed.

"I can ask what he wants to donate," Ruth said. Usually they just gave money, not an auction item.

"This year is going to be different. I am going to try to get businesses to donate time as well as stuff. Like I want Tess to donate her time as a financial planner, so her item would be a day of free financial advice."

"It's not really free if they had to buy the person at the auction. Besides, she is the bank's president, not a financial advisor," Ruth said.

"But she was a financial advisor before becoming a bank president. She can spend a day at it again. I think she still remembers how to do it." Mia leaned back in her chair again.

"Do you want Anderson to give a day of insurance advice? He does that all the time for free, so he won't draw in a lot of money."

"I was thinking Anderson could probably just donate this year. I can't even auction him off for a date," Mia grinned.

"No, you can't," Ruth agreed and laughed with Mia, loving that he was hers this year, at least for a time.

"I'll put you down for cash." Mia pulled out her phone and typed the information on it.

Just then, Anderson walked into the office. Ruth looked at the clock and then at him in puzzlement. It was only ten after the hour. The funeral must have just started.

"Hey, Anderson," Mia greeted him. "Just got you down for money for the flood auction."

"Okay." He nodded but wasn't really into the conversation. "Ruth, grab your coat. We are going for a ride."

Mia could see that she wasn't needed as a distraction and had gotten what she wanted for her auction, so she got up and said her goodbyes and left them alone. Ruth watched her go out into the warm day. She was, of course, not wearing a coat. Ruth turned back to Anderson but didn't say anything, just sat there.

"Come on, you need to get out of town. Let's go." He came around the desk and held his hand out to her.

"Where are we going?" she asked, not taking his hand.

"Out of town. I am taking you out for supper in Grand Forks."

She looked at the clock on the wall. It was just after two o'clock. "We will be early for supper."

"Come on, Ruth. Let's go," he said again, grabbing her hand and pulling her to her feet. Once she was standing, he kept pulling until she was in his arms. "You need to get your mind off today."

His mouth was then on hers, warming her from the inside out. She hadn't realized how cold she had been. Running her hands up his warm chest, feeling the muscles under her fingers, she forgot they were in front of the window facing Main Street. Or maybe she didn't care anymore.

As his lips raised from hers, he whispered, "Let's get changed and get out of here." And he pulled away from her and out of the office. Shutting off the lights and locking the door, they headed upstairs, away from life for the day.

An hour later, Ruth was watching the snow piles in yards and in the fields as they drove south. It had taken longer than planned to get changed because Anderson had insisted on finishing what they had started downstairs.

Now he was in his brown sweater that matched his eyes, and he looked good. Since they had started to spend more time together, she had gotten to see him in more casual clothing, and she really liked it. Not that he didn't look good at the office, but jeans were great at showing off his butt.

Curling her feet under her in the large cab of his pickup, she asked, "Where are we going for supper?"

Turning, he put a hand on her knee that was nearest to him. "To my mom's."

Her smiled faded. "What?"

"I saw where you came from. I thought I would show you where I came from," he said as he drove down the road, barreling towards his mom's house.

"I don't know if you want them to meet me. I mean, I am nothing they want to know." She stumbled over her words. Sure, he had met her mom, but were they really at this stage?

"My mom has been asking for weeks. Dad not so much, but he knows about you." He squeezed her knee a little in reassurance.

"You told them?"

"Of course. I like you, Ruth. I want you to meet my parents."

"But won't your dad be mad? I work for you." She knew there was no rule about it, but he was the boss's son. Sometimes there were different rules for them.

"He is okay with it. There are rules about dating in the office at the main office, but not at the branches," he explained, which meant that he had already told his dad about them. But what exactly did he say?

"Will your brother be there?" Another thought crossed her mind. What if Jonathan told his dad about her? What if he told his dad a different version of what happened when he came to visit? Will his dad, the owner, dislike her?

"Probably not. Not after what happened at the office," Anderson replied.

"I wish you would have told me; I would have put something nicer on." She looked at the old jeans and light blue sweater she was wearing. Maybe she should have put on makeup or done something with her hair, something to make her look better.

"You look beautiful, Ruth. I wouldn't change anything about you. My parents are going to love you." He ran a hand across her back and under her hair, caressing her neck.

"I do want to see where you came from," Ruth admitted, settling into the idea of meeting his parents. It wasn't like she could stop it now.

"Not a cute little farm. I grew up in town. Oddly, my parents have kept the same house all these years." He smiled at her.

"I didn't grow up on a farm. Mom married Chester, who had the farm. Before that, we lived in Mia's apartment. I have almost always lived downtown."

"So, you've only moved across the road?" he asked.

"Yes. It might explain why I am content downtown; it's my neighborhood." Though as a child, she had hated being the only kid downtown. Maybe that's why she played with Rafferty. He was with his dad during the summers at the office.

"This is my parents'." Anderson waved at the big houses and big yards. She could almost see kids playing in the yards and riding bikes down the road. She wished she could see it in summer instead of covered in piles of deep snow.

After pulling up to a gray house, Anderson shut off the car as Ruth looked around. As she opened the door, the cool air circled around her, her sweater providing little protection against the weather.

Anderson walked around the car and took her hand. He must have noticed how nervous she was because he pulled her into his arms and said, "Don't be nervous. They are going to love you."

He held her hand as they walked up to the door and went inside. It was twice the size of the home her mother owned and maybe even bigger than that. Looking up at the two-story entry, she wondered why someone would need something so grand.

He called out a greeting as they slipped off their shoes by the entry door. Turning, she saw an older couple coming her way. The man looked a lot like Jonathan, only older. The woman, who was smiling at her, had Anderson's coloring. Ruth liked her immediately.

She smiled as Anderson introduced her to Dan and Kim Miles, his parents. To her surprise, they did seem happy to be introduced to her. His mom even gave her a hug.

"I am so happy Andy finally brought you to meet us." Dan slapped his son on the back. Though Ruth had worked for his company for over four years, she had never met the man. Occasionally, she had talked to him on the phone.

"I didn't realize he was hiding me." She gave a nervous laugh.

"Maybe not hiding, but keeping you to himself," Kim said as she led her towards the kitchen in the back of the house. It was through a living room that looked like it wasn't used and through a dining room with placemats already set on the long shiny table.

"You have a beautiful home, Mrs. Miles," she commented as they finally entered the gourmet kitchen.

"Thank you. You can call me Kim, please. Can I call you Ruth?" She ushered her to the island to sit on a stool. Anderson followed and sat next to her.

"Yes, please."

"You don't hear that name so much in young people today," Kim said as she poured waters for everyone.

"No, you don't. I was named after my mother's grandmother. Her name was also Mary Ruth." She nodded in thanks for the drink as Kim sat down. She could feel Anderson's eyes on her. She couldn't remember if she told him that before.

"It's pretty," Kim said, smiling.

"So, you work for Andy?" Dan asked. He was leaning against the cabinets near his wife.

"Yes, I have worked for Anderson for five years now, but I have worked in the office for almost a dozen." Ruth took a drink, hoping they stopped asking about the office. Maybe they would realize right away how little she did for Anderson.

"Has it been an insurance office the entire time?" Kim asked, interested.

"Yes. Before Anderson, I worked for Frank Berg the entire time. He always sold insurance."

"But you never thought about selling?" Dan asked.

Anderson chuckled beside her as if his dad had told a joke. Did he think that the idea of her selling insurance was preposterous? That she wasn't smart enough?

"No, I never really was interested in it. I know quite a bit about the whole industry, but I am happy that Anderson took over the claims process. Frank always made me type those out for him. They are the reason I have such fast typing speeds." She chuckled at the memory of those long days after a storm of just typing out report after report. Eight hours were a dream in those days.

"You had to fill those out? I don't let anyone but the agent fill those out," Dan said.

"They are easy once you get used to the process. For me, the harder part is when people call with complaints saying that their claims are too low or their deductibles are too high. Explaining that is always harder," she told Dan.

Anderson stiffened beside her. "I don't get complaint calls."

"Don't worry, Anderson," she said, turning to him. "I have taken care of them, and there's hardly any now. People are used to you."

"I have never gotten a call about that stuff," Anderson argued.

"I know, your personal assistant takes care of it. That's her job." Ruth tapped him on the leg.

"Looks like your personal assistant is doing her job, Andy," Dan said with a laugh.

Anderson glanced at her, remembering that she really didn't do much for him. Guilt swamped her, and she fell silent as Anderson started to talk to his dad about insurance stuff.

Kim leaned over to her as the men talked and said, "Do you always call him Anderson?"

She looked up at his mom, puzzled. "Yes, it's his name."

"I know, but everyone calls him Andy. It seems sweet that you call him Anderson."

"I guess a lot of people in Landstad call him Anderson. I never even knew that he had a nickname until recently," Ruth admitted.

"We need to go out there sometime. I mean, it's not that far," Kim said, looking at her husband.

"You should. It's a great town, and you can see where Anderson lives and works," Ruth replied, knowing that the couple would love the little town—most people did.

"Do you have a house in town, Ruth?" Kim asked her.

"No, Mom, she doesn't have a house. She actually rents downtown above the office." Ruth looked over at him. He made it sound like she had no attachments to her place, that he was more stable because he had a house with a yard. Yet she was the one who owned her home, not him.

"At least her commute is short, especially in the winter." Dan chuckled.

"Is it a nice place, Ruth?" Kim asked.

Anderson jumped in to answer again. "It's just a little place. Nice, but just a two-bedroom."

Ruth looked over at him in shock. He said her place was just a little apartment, nothing special. Her place was two apartments made into one before she moved into it. It was actually the largest place in the entire downtown area, she should know. And considering the place across the hallway, she had more square feet than many homes in Landstad; more importantly, more than he himself had. It stung that he thought so little of the place she loved.

"It's a nice place. I have always liked it," she mumbled to the couple in front of her.

Before anyone could comment, the front door opened, and someone called out like Anderson had. Ruth's heart stopped. It was Jonathan, she was sure of it. Though she had only talked to him a few times, his voice was very recognizable.

He came into the kitchen, pushing a petite brunette carrying a baby. Looking over the woman, Ruth realized how different she was from Anderson's first love. The woman before her was every bit the professional's wife, and she was beautiful. Her smile captivated the room, and everyone turned to her as she said hello. Ruth suddenly felt old, plain, and frumpy.

She watched as Noel gave Anderson a hug, and with a wispy voice, the brunette said, "Good to see you, Andy."

Anderson only had eyes for the woman with the baby in her arms. Once she had entered the room, Anderson's hand on her thigh had dropped. With the new couple in the room, Anderson seemed to have had forgotten that Ruth was even there for all the attention he paid her, and she was right beside him.

CHAPTER 20

ANDERSON HUGGED HIS SISTER-IN-LAW. He didn't see her much since he stopped coming to Grand Forks every weekend. She was just as beautiful as she had been when he had met her and brought her home from college to meet his parents. But since that day, he had lost interest in her. She was just his brother's wife now and had been for years. Glancing at Ruth, he wondered if his feelings for her would fade like that. But oddly, he knew they would not. He didn't even think that they would ever dim.

Noel handed the baby to Anderson and turned to Ruth. "I am Noel. You must be Ruth. When Kim said Andy was bringing you over today, I knew I had to see who had captivated Andy so much."

"Nice to meet you too." Ruth smiled as she said it, but Anderson could tell she was in her prim and proper secretary mode now. Her emotions were closed, and he couldn't understand why.

"And this is my husband, Jonathan." Noel pointed at the man holding a three-year-old little girl who looked more like her mother than her father.

"We have met," was all Ruth said, but her tone made Jonathan go pale. He could see his brother had taken her threat seriously, which was a good thing.

"Supper is almost ready, so why don't you guys go set the table in the dining room, and us girls will get everything ready?" His mom sensed the tension and was trying to defuse it.

His mother's idea didn't work. The tension was still there as the roast and potatoes were served. Ruth was able to keep up with the conversation going around the table better than he could. All he could think was that he had done something wrong to change her mood. After they were done eating, he draped his hand over Ruth's chair and rubbed her back with his fingers. He felt the tension in her body, and she pulled away from his touch.

They said goodbye to everyone and headed out, making excuses about the drive. The tension followed them into the car, and he wondered if anyone else had noticed it. Maybe because he knew her moods, he noticed that hers had changed so completely from when they had first arrived.

As the miles slipped by, the pickup cab was silent, except for the radio playing quietly. As town drew close, he asked, "What is the matter, Ruth?"

"Nothing." She would not look at him.

"Is it Jonathan? Did he do or stay something?"

"No, he wouldn't do or say anything in front of his wife or dad." She shot him an angry look.

"What then?"

"You don't know, do you?"

"Apparently not."

Turning back to the window, she quietly replied, "Once Noel came in the room, you forgot I was there. All your attention was on her."

"I never forget you are there," he assured her.

She was focusing on the fields outside her window when she again whispered, "You are ashamed of me."

"Why would you ever think I am ashamed of you?"

"You didn't want to introduce me to someone you used to love." She looked out the dark window, still not meeting his eyes.

"She did it before I could. Noel is just that way. She takes over when she comes in. I am just so used to it that I let it happen. I am sorry." He hoped she would forgive him for his lapse, but it really was how Noel had always been. It was why she and Jonathan were a perfect match.

"You don't think I do anything at the office. I know I don't work all day, but I do everything you ask of me and everything that needs to be done," she accused.

"I know you do a lot. You are just so efficient that I don't notice it," he argued back.

"You laughed at the thought that I could be smart enough to sell insurance. I am surprised you didn't tell them I barely graduated from high school or that I am stupid." She turned to him with her hurt blue eyes.

"You have never given any indication that you would be interested in selling insurance. You even said yourself you didn't want to sell it." He pulled up in front of her apartment.

"Maybe I would one day, but you don't think I can. Then you made fun of my apartment as if you need to own grass for it to be a home. I think I have made my place a home. It has more square footage than that place you rent," she insisted.

"How would you know? You have never been there," he questioned, letting her anger get the better of him.

"I have too," she hissed.

"Once." And they hadn't stayed long.

"I don't know why you want to drive four blocks when I live upstairs. No warming up a car, no wasted time."

"I have to admit, your place is convenient, but my place is nice too," he pushed.

"You rent. How is that better than my apartment?" she demanded.

"It's normal, Ruth, to live in a house. That's normal."

"Your normal and mine are completely different, Anderson." Ruth's tone had gone flat, no longer was she fighting with him, she was stating facts.

"Ruth."

"This is your normal, Anderson: a happy house in a happy neighborhood where your friends lived, where you rode your bikes up and down the sidewalks. My normal is living in my crappy apartment. This isn't going to work. We are too different to keep trying." She pulled the door handle, and the dome light turned on, but she didn't open the door to the cold night air.

"What?" He looked into her light blue eyes.

"This. Us." She pushed open the door and climbed out of the cab.

The door slammed behind her, and he watched her enter her apartment. Had she just broken up with him? Is that what had just happened? Jumping out of the pickup, he hurried after her running up her now familiar stairs. Kicking off his shoes in the hallway, he first looked into the office to see if she had gone to hide in there. It was her go-to hiding place, but it was empty.

Opening the apartment door, he yelled, "Ruth, where are you?"

Oddly, he didn't need to have yelled because she was in the kitchen a few feet from him. He was so used to her rushing to the back of the apartment to change clothes the moment she was home that her being in the kitchen still in jeans and a sweater seemed odd. In her hand was a bottle of whiskey, and she had pulled a glass down from the cabinet but had not had time yet to pour the liquid.

"Ruth Kennedy, I am not letting you break up with me for being different." He stalked over to her and took the bottle out of her hands and put it on the counter. Trapping her between his arms, he looked into those ice-blue eyes. "Us being different is what makes it so great. That you are different from me. That your apartment is above the office. That when you are up here, I can picture what you are doing. And I love that you sit at that desk down there and read words that you wrote right above my head."

He stopped and watched her eyes as they stared back at him. Her breathing was faster than normal. "I can never get a word in when Noel is there; she dominates conversations. Yes, I brought her home from college, but I never loved her. Yes, I like her as a sister-in-law, but that is it. I wanted to introduce her to the woman I am in love with, but I just couldn't get a word in."

Lowering his mouth until it almost touched hers, he whispered, "I am in love with *you*, Ruth Kennedy."

He felt her breath catch at his words. His hands left the counter and wrapped around her, and she went willingly. Her arms went around him, and he knew that her anger was gone.

Lifting her into his arms, he carried her into the bedroom. If he wasn't kissing her still, he would have laughed that the bed was still rumpled from when they had made love before leaving for his parent's house. Nothing was distracting him from this woman tonight.

CHAPTER 21

ANOTHER SUNDAY NIGHT of book club had Anderson out of Ruth's place and back at his own for an evening. It was quiet and lonely on the nights he stayed there. This was the first book club night since he had told her he loved her. Though she had not returned the words, he was sure she loved him just as much. Even if the words her mom had said still rattled around his mind, he knew his love for her was enough to keep them together.

Since he had hours on his hands, he decided to grab some boxes and start packing up his stuff. Maybe it was too soon, but he hoped to move in with Ruth. Once he talked to her about it, he was hoping to move fast—no more of this her place/his place stuff.

Just as he had the first box half full of books, his dad called him. It was rare that his dad called; it was usually his mom. For his entire life, he had been closer to his mom, while Jonathan was closer to their dad. Wondering what would make his dad call from out of the blue, Anderson sat on the couch and listened to his dad in shock.

The older man jumped right in with his thought that it was time to have Anderson move back to Grand Forks. Dan was opening a new branch and wanted his son in charge of it—not at the home office, but his own branch in the city. Anderson had no idea what to say about the offer. Would Ruth go with him? His father had sweetened the deal by saying that Ruth should be brought on board and trained to become an agent if she wanted to. If not, she could still work for Anderson in any capacity she wanted. Dan had been so impressed by her the night she had met him that he thought that she would excel as an agent. They both agreed that she was wasted as a personal assistant.

When Anderson had asked about the Landstad branch, his dad had informed him that he, Anderson, could pick the person to replace him if he knew anyone interested. His mind went immediately to Rafferty. It would be perfect to have him move over. Then he wouldn't have to worry about leaving this office with someone he didn't know. Or someone who didn't know the town.

Anderson chatted for a while longer with his dad. His dad said he should talk to Rafferty and Ruth, and Dan himself would contact the rental company to change the lease on the building. It seemed like something Anderson could handle, but he was happy his dad was going to do it. It showed him that his dad was serious about everything.

Anderson was too keyed-up to sleep, and Ruth hadn't texted yet that the girls were gone, so he called Rafferty about it. "Rafferty, I just talked to my dad about me opening a branch in Grand Forks. What do you think of working at the Landstad branch?"

Rafferty was silent for a bit before asking, "What does Angel say?"

"I haven't talked to her yet. It's book club tonight, and I just got off the phone with dad," Anderson explained.

"What about Angel?" Rafferty asked, in the last few weeks Anderson had noticed it was more of a term of endearment then a spiteful nickname from her past.

"My dad is offering to train her to be an agent. She will train in my new branch." He hoped she would be excited.

"I don't know, Anderson. I don't think Angel will move. She is a Tiger." Rafferty did not sound as happy about it as he had a few minutes before.

"What exactly is a Tiger?" he demanded, having never once heard of it.

"Someone who lives in Landstad forever. Never moves, never wants to," Rafferty explained, though it still made no sense to Anderson. "Take my word for it. She is a Tiger."

The words reminded Anderson of all the times she had stated that she would not leave. But that was before she had a job away from Landstad, a far better job than the one she had here. That was before they were in love.

"I think I know her better than you," Anderson argued. She would see how much better it would be in Grand Forks. With a new job, a new house, a new life.

"I don't think you do, Anderson. Do you know that she gives money to any organization in town who asks her?" Rafferty said from out of nowhere.

"The agency money?"

"No, Anderson, she gives her own money. Sports teams, charities, fundraisers... I think she gives big time at the spring auction," Rafferty stated.

"Why would she do that?" Anderson leaned back on the couch in confusion.

"Because she loves this town. It's her town. I don't see her leaving it."

His friend didn't know Ruth enough. They might have grown up together, but they were not close anymore.

"I am going to talk to her first thing in the morning about it. I can't interrupt book club night. You will see I know her a little better than you do." Anderson said goodbye and stared at the phone.

Why would she not leave this little place? Grand Forks was exciting and fun. There was nothing to do here. Her job was a dead end that she barely actually worked at. They would do so much better in the city than here.

Giving up on packing for the night, he turned on the TV and watched a few episodes of a show that was funny enough to take his mind off the morning and his talk with Ruth. By the time he went to bed, he knew she would be just as excited about the move as he was.

He wondered if the girls were still at Ruth's place or if he could go over there and talk to her now. But there had been no text yet, so they must still be there. Or they left too late for her to think he would come back to her place, not realizing it was never too late to spend the night with her.

CHAPTER 22

MIA WAS TELLING the book club about how the auction planning was going. Tess was ignoring her because she kept saying how great it was that Tess was going to be auctioned off. Mia not-so-secretly hoped it would have been a bachelor/bachelorette auction and that all the couples would fall in love, all because of Mia. Since Mia was also drunk, she said it out loud to everyone. Everyone laughed, except Tess, who was already signed up to be auctioned off.

"Anyone want more?" Ruth asked from the counter that held all the alcohol. Nobody responded, so she took her glass back over to the table and sat down. The night was winding down.

"How is the great romance going?" Natalie asked. Natalie was currently engaged with a summer wedding and wanted everyone to be in love.

"Great. I think we met each other's parents in the last few weeks," Ruth admitted.

"Ohhhh!" Mandy Nordskov said loudly.

"How is it that you only *think* it happened? It either did, or it didn't." Mia finished her drink.

"He drove me out to see my mom one day, and then a few days later, we went and had supper with his parents. Neither meeting was great, but we will move on from there." Ruth didn't tell them exactly why it had happened and didn't go into details. Now that it was over, she was happy to be done with those stressful activities. Meeting each other's parents should be a happy time and not be overshadowed by a funeral or what had happened in her mom's kitchen.

"Is he moving in yet?" Tess raised an eyebrow in question.

"We haven't talked about it." Ruth smiled at her but secretly hoped it would happen soon. He was there all the time, anyway. He had some stuff at her place already, but she wanted all of his stuff and all of him living with her.

"You should," Natalie agreed.

"Is he staying here? In Landstad, I mean, because the entire town knows he is staying in this apartment," Mia asked. It seemed more like she was trying to get gossip from her, but that might've been because she was quite drunk.

"Probably not forever." Ruth knew the answer, though she tried not to think about it. She was sure he would leave one day.

"Will you go with him?" Hazel asked. She was usually the quiet one in the group, and Ruth was happy she was joining the conversation, even if she didn't want to talk about herself.

"No, I will stay here. I don't want to leave," Ruth told everyone.

"Why not? There's nothing here." Mia got up to pour herself another glass, though she really didn't need it.

"I get it, Ruth," Tess said. "It's a neat little town, the people are nice, and it sometimes just feels like home."

"Thank you, Tess." She smiled at the woman.

"Can't it feel like home somewhere else with Anderson?" Natalie asked.

"I don't know. I like it here," Ruth argued.

"You might have to decide if you like it here more than you like being with Anderson," Mandy stated. As usual, she was the adult in the room.

"Maybe one day." Ruth drank her mixed drink.

"Well, tomorrow comes early," Mia said, standing up as she

finished her drink. Mia was usually at the café before six in the morning, no matter how much she drank the night before.

"Good thing you are not driving. I wonder if you are going to make it across the street," Tess said to their neighbor.

"I will make sure she gets across the street," Hazel said and followed Mia out of the apartment.

"I have to go too. I've got wedding invites to address. It is easier when you are a bit buzzed," Natalie said as she packed up her computer. Ruth and Tess helped by packing up the headphones to put in the box Natalie brought back and forth.

"I will carry her box out. No need for Natalie to take two trips." Tess grabbed the box and headed for the door after Natalie.

After saying goodbye as her friends headed out for the evening, she shut the door after them. Ruth glanced at the clock; it was just before eight o'clock. Maybe she should call Anderson to come over.

Ruth forced herself to clean the house first. Quickly, she put the alcohol away, and the pop and juices were then put in the fridge. After putting the glasses in the dishwasher, she grabbed her phone. After snuggling into the couch, she saw she had a text.

Sadly, it wasn't from Anderson. It was from her rental agency who dealt with her tenants. Opening the text, she read that they had sent her an email. Must be a contract. They always emailed those to her. It was easier to print and file from an email.

With a groan, she got up and crossed over to her office and turned on her computer. Better to look at it on the big screen than on her phone in case it was something serious.

Opening the email, her heart sank as she read the words in front of her. It was the rental agreement for this building, and it changed the renter from Anderson Miles to Rafferty Brooks. She had a clause in all her agreements that if the person who rented it changed, there would be a new agreement written up. And here it was.

Anderson was leaving, and he hadn't told her. The fact that he was leaving was heart-wrenching enough, but him not telling her was as bad as Franky leaving her years before.

Based on the date, he would be gone in two weeks. How long had he been planning this? Was he ever going to tell her? Did he think she wouldn't notice when Rafferty came to work instead of him?

After printing the contract, she opened a new document. The resignation letter was brief and to the point; no flowery words were needed. She printed that one too. With both papers printed, her hand shook as she signed them both. Along with her signature, Anderson was leaving her life.

When they had started dating, she had known it would end but felt they had more time. Instead, they had a matter of weeks before he would be gone. After so many years of pining after him, she only got to hold on to him for a blink of an eye.

Taking the papers, she slipped on her shoes and walked down to the office. Turning on the light, she put each paper in a folder and placed them on Anderson's desk. From there, she went to her desk and turned on the computer. As she waited, she removed anything personal that she wanted. There was nothing; she had no pictures, no knickknacks, nothing. Twelve years, and nothing was hers in the office...except the office itself.

Once the computer was on, she wiped the computer back to the basic programs and a few insurance ones that were needed. Then she changed the networking information to a basic network that joined the two computers. She did the same with Anderson's computer.

On her way out of the office, she looked around at where she had spent so many hours. Had they been wasted in this office? It would never be the same without Anderson.

Remembering the first day he had shown up, she had wondered if she should have quit when Frank did. When Anderson had walked through the door, she knew she had to stay, to see where this would all lead to. Five years later, and now she knew it went nowhere.

Grabbing her name plaque from the desk, she shut off the light and locked the door behind her. The cold air swirled around her as she touched the door where his name was printed on it. Anderson Miles.

Back upstairs, she called her mom, who did not ask any questions.

Instead, she just said she would come for her. At that point, she had twenty minutes before her mom got there.

First, she dismantled her computers from her office and put them in a box. She would take them both and three important pieces of network equipment from the wall. One cordless headset was added to the pile, and everything was placed by the door. Next, she went to her bedroom. Taking out the old suitcase that she had used only a few times, she packed it until it was full, then called it done. If she didn't have it, she didn't need it.

With the few remaining minutes, she emptied her fridge of things that would be rotten in the two weeks before April first, Anderson's last day in Landstad. She emptied the garbage and put it in the hallway as well.

Before leaving, Ruth looked around her apartment one last time. It looked clean and comfortable. It looked like her home. She would be back in a month, but she couldn't watch Anderson walk out of her life. She wasn't strong enough for that, not again.

Quickly she took the garbage out to the dumpster in the back of the building and then started to move her boxes down the stairs. Soon, her mom showed up to help, and Chester, too. The three of them silently moved all the boxes to her mom's Buick's massive trunk and back seat.

Sara handed her daughter the keys to the old car and gave her a long hug. Ruth fought back the tears as she watched her mom climb into the passenger seat next to Chester. Then they drove off. They would head back to where they came from.

Ruth locked the door to her apartment for the first time in years, then climbed into the car that was still warm from her mom driving it to her. As she headed out of town, she let the tears fall. Anderson had forced her out of the town she loved, or was it really that she loved Anderson, and he was leaving town? Leaving her.

CHAPTER 23

RUTH WAS LATE. Anderson was already pacing the office. She was fifteen minutes late. It was the morning after book club, so he usually didn't worry about her tardiness, but this was later than she had ever been. He had texted her that morning before he had come in to see how she was doing, but he hadn't gotten a text back. That in itself was unusual.

The bell over the door chimed, and Anderson turned, hoping to see Ruth, but it was only Rafferty. A smiling Rafferty.

"No, Angel today?" Rafferty looked at the empty desk in confusion.

"She's just running late."

"Angel?"

"Yeah, can you watch the office? I am going to run up there and see what is going on."

"Sure." Rafferty sat down at Ruth's desk chair, spinning it around as he did.

But Anderson didn't wait for him to answer before he was out the door and down to her glass door. He went to yank it open and almost dislocated his arm as the door stayed shut. Trying again, he realized it was locked. Looking closer through the glass, he saw nothing unusual in the stairway. But the door was locked, so something was up.

Back in the office, Rafferty was still sitting at Ruth's desk. He had the computer on and was looking through the drawers. "Is there a key in there? The door is locked."

"Angel's door? The street door? In Landstad?" Rafferty started to look through the desk as he asked the questions. Looking around, he shook his head and closed the drawer.

"I know. I have never seen it locked before either. She won't answer my texts." He took out his phone and called her number and listened to it ring. It went to voice mail, and he left another message.

In front of him, Rafferty had his phone out and was calling someone as well, but his call was answered. "Mia, have you heard from Ruth today?"

Either Anderson didn't hear an answer, or there was no answer because Rafferty lowered his phone and set it on the desk. His friend was looking around the office as if he was looking for the answer to where she was in the room.

He watched Mia run across the street from the café without even looking for traffic in the street. She also tried the glass door. Then she came over to the office and slammed her way in. Her eyes jumped from man to man as she demanded, "What have you done?"

"Me?" Anderson asked, utterly confused.

She turned to Rafferty. "You?"

"Nothing. Haven't talked to her in a few weeks." Rafferty had his hands in the air as if that would show his innocence.

"Then I say it was you, Anderson. She was fine last night. Happy and fine. What happened?" Mia had her hands on her hips and was staring at him.

"I haven't talked to her since I left when book club started last night."

"What did you do last night?" Folding her arms she glared at him not giving up on him being the issue.

"I was home all night," Anderson said.

"You called me," Rafferty offered as he turned on the computer in front of him. Anderson nearly stopped him from doing it. It seemed like an invasion of her privacy to have him looking at her computer, especially when he knew what Ruth did most of the day on that computer.

"I talked to my dad, and I talked to Rafferty. Nothing was said that would upset Ruth. I don't even know how she would know what we talked about to upset her."

Mia was not letting it go. "You did something."

"Doesn't Ruth have a background on her computer that is a picture of that window in the summer?" Rafferty asked as he looked at the computer.

"Yes, she changes it to the opposite season." It was a cute quirk he had noticed years before.

"It's not on the computer anymore."

Anderson went over to her computer and saw that over half the icons that were usually on it were gone. Something had happened to her computer over the weekend. Going into his office, he turned on his computer to see he had the same issue. Sitting in the chair, he waited for the computer to warm up. He started tapping impatiently on his desk and noticed an unlabeled folder. As the computer did its thing, he opened the file. It contained a contract for the rent of this office. It was made out with Rafferty's name where his used to be.

Closing his eyes, he realized the contract was accidentally sent to the office, and she had found it this morning. She knew he was leaving, and she was gone. No not gone. She was up in her office, which was why the door was locked. To keep him out.

Throwing the file back onto the desk, but it slipped onto the floor. That was when he saw another just like it still on the desk. Opening it, he knew what this one would say. It was a neatly typed resignation letter. She had quit.

Anderson jumped up from his desk and went into the supply room and grabbed a hammer. Rushing back out of the office, he almost ran over Mia as he headed out the door. Both Rafferty and Mia were on his heels when he stopped at her locked door. He tried it one more time, but it was still locked.

With a loud crash, the hammer went through the glass of the door.

Carefully, he unlocked the door and went up the stairs to find her. She was there. He knew she was there; he just had to find her.

The three of them made it to the landing. Mia went into the apartment. It looked as it always did; nothing was missing but her purse. Mia went to the bedroom and said she thought all of Ruth's clothes were there as if she would know.

Anderson turned and went across the hall, but that door was locked as well. She was in there—there was no other place she could be. With a firm kick, the door flew open. He expected to see her sitting behind her desk with headphones on, but he looked around the little apartment, seeing she wasn't there. In fact, most of her computer system was gone, both computers and a bunch of other stuff.

"What is this?" Mia asked, looking around.

"This is her office. She took the computers. She's gone this time," Anderson said.

"Why?" Rafferty asked, looking around the little apartment. His eyes were on the furniture that was there, not the missing computer equipment, the important stuff.

"She was accidentally sent the new rental contract with Rafferty's name on it. My dad offered me a branch in Grand Forks. I was asking her to come with me. He was offering her a job, also."

"You are a moron! She's never going to leave Landstad, she is a tiger!" Mia yelled at him, saying the same thing Rafferty had the night before. What was it about this town?

"I think she would leave. She has nothing here but her mom!" Anderson defended loudly.

"She has everything she has ever wanted here, even if you don't want any of it," Mia insisted.

"I thought that love would be enough," Anderson stated.

"Maybe if you had just talked to her about it." Rafferty made it sound like he was an expert at relationships.

"I was going to today. Why did they have to send her the contract? One small mistake was all it took." He shook his head at the mix-up.

"The same reason I come into your office every month, Anderson. The same reason she lives here in this building. Did you even read the contract, Anderson?" Mia kicked at the wall and walked out of the smaller apartment.

Watching her made him wonder what Mia knew that he didn't. The woman knew everything about this town, but he thought he knew all of Ruth's secrets.

Rafferty walked around the shabby room. "She left Landstad?"

"She ran away, just like Ruth always does," Anderson hissed out.

"No, this would be the first time she has ever done that. She's coming back once you are gone. Tigers come back." Rafferty walked out of the office and into the hallway.

"What is that supposed to mean?" Anderson yelled at him.

"It means that once you leave this town in the dust, she will come back. She hasn't run off; she is letting you leave without having to watch you leave her behind," Rafferty turned and said.

"I was *not* leaving her behind!" Anderson yelled.

"Yes, you were. You were leaving, and she was never going to follow!" Rafferty yelled back as he went down the stairs to the street level.

Following, Anderson knew Rafferty was right. They had all been right. Ruth had told him on day one of their relationship and even at his parents' house that she was staying here. There was nothing that would make her move, not even him. He had been the one who couldn't believe it.

As Rafferty stomped off to his pickup, Anderson went back into the office. The silence was deafening. He missed her constant typing, missed her sitting behind her desk. He missed everything about her.

Going into his office, he picked up the files he had thrown on the floor earlier. He put them back on his desk and sat in his chair, trying not to look over at her empty chair. He had two weeks to look at that empty chair.

When the bell tinkled over the door, he jumped out of his chair and rushed to the door, only to stop when he saw Tess Thorn walk into the room. She lived next door, right next to Ruth.

"Was there a break-in? Is Ruth okay?" Tess indicated towards the broken door.

"No, I did that. She left."

"Left? To where?"

"I don't know." He slumped back in his chair. "She quit."

"What did you do?" Tess asked the same question Mia had. What was it about her friends to think he was always in the wrong? Except she was right.

"I am leaving, going back to Grand Forks. I foolishly wanted her to go with me," Anderson confessed.

"You're right that was foolish, Anderson. This is where she wants to be. She has never given me any indication she wanted to leave. The complete opposite, in fact. She has too much going on here to actually walk away." Tess sat down in the chair across from him.

"There is nothing for her in this town. She has rented that place upstairs for over a dozen years. Has she ever even thought about buying a house? She wastes money on charity that she could invest." He watched as Tess looked through the files with the rental contract and resignation letter. He didn't even care.

"Did you ever talk to her about it? Her wasting money, that is?" Tess questioned.

"No," he admitted. He hadn't wanted to bring up money. The only time they ever talked about it was in the context of how badly she was paid by him.

"It's her money to waste or invest as she sees fit. From what I have seen from her portfolio at the bank, she is pretty conservative with her money."

"You know how much money she has?" He was surprised at her admission.

She just shrugged. "Yes, she is a bank client. Recently, she moved some money around, so I looked through her portfolio. It is my job."

"Every month, she wastes money on rent when she could be paying a mortgage and getting some return on her money," he argued. She was a banker; she should know all this.

"You rent, Anderson, both your home and this office. Which means you are wasting money times two."

"We are not talking about me. Did you see that she quit her job?" Anderson nodded at the resignation letter in her hand.

He watched Tess look over it again. It was short, and the bank president read it quickly. "I am actually happy she quit. She should have left a long time ago. This job was just a waste of her time."

Anderson looked at the woman across from him. "You know what she does?"

"No, I just know that you don't pay her enough. A pittance, Anderson. Her income comes from other locations."

"Income?" he questioned the word choice.

"Seriously, Anderson, I thought you were practically living with the woman?" Tess said, opening the other file in her hand and taking out the rental agreement. With both papers, she laid them on the table in front of him. "You didn't even see that she signed these wrong."

Looking down at the papers in front of him, he saw for the first time that the resignation letter was signed M Johnson, and the rental agreement was signed Ruth Kennedy. He saw a glimmer of hope. "These are not legal then."

"They are legal, Anderson. She can sign either one of them any way she wants. Her name is Mary Ruth Johnson Kennedy. It's still Ruth who signed them." She got up to leave, dropping the papers back on the desk.

He didn't even look up when she asked, "Why would she sign a rental agreement?"

Tess stopped at the door. "Because Ruth owns this building and has been its owner for as long as you have been here. She also owns the building I live in, the one Mia lives in, Rafferty's building, a few others downtown, and a few rental houses around town, including yours. Ruth has slowly bought up this town and now has a major share of it."

Anderson watched her walk out of the office and turn towards the bank. Could she be right that Ruth owned buildings in this town? This building? Every year he had her write a letter to the owner about how cold it gets in the office during the winter. He remembered her face when she told him that the owner always reads his complaints. Why didn't she say anything?

Most likely because he treated her like a personal assistant that had no ambitions and no future. Like he had so much to offer that she couldn't get on her own…that he was smarter than she was.

For the first time, he wondered how much money she made from writing. When she had first told him about it, he had thought it was a fun hobby to keep her busy. Now he realized that her hobby was actually her real job. No, she had said she loved her work but enjoyed her job. Now he knew that working with him had only been her job, not her career.

At that moment, he finally realized that he had to decide if he was going to give up his dream of working in Grand Forks to stay with her. This morning, he had to convince her that she loved him enough to move with him. Now he had to decide if he loved her enough to stay.

Everyone who knew her knew she wasn't leaving, that this is where she wanted to stay. This town was the most important thing to her.

CHAPTER 24

THE SNOW WAS ALMOST GONE from the parking lot as Ruth loaded another box of computer equipment into the back of the car. Well, it wasn't a car; it was a cute little SUV. Within a week of moving into the apartment in Grand Forks, her mom had taken her car back, but in the bigger town, Ruth wasn't able to get around like she wanted and had gone and purchased her first brand-new car. After taking a cab to the dealership, she had bought the one she liked the best. It was a dark brown on the outside and inside, and the color reminded her of Anderson's eyes.

In the month she had been away, she had spent most of it in her new apartment. On the drive to town that night, she had contacted her rental agency, and they had found her a place she would be able to get in that night. It was small and furnished, but that suited her just fine. She had set up her computers on the dining room table and had lost herself in the worlds that she created. Worlds where everyone was happy in the end.

Finally able to write like never before, she saw how much time she wasted on work and everything that entailed. Just showering every day had cost her a chapter, based on her actual output this month—though she had to shower once in a while.

What made it different in a bigger town was that she could order food at any time. Anything she wanted and at any time. The first week she had lost writing time just looking at menus. Since then, she had ordered from nearly every restaurant in town that delivered.

Another of her new habits was that she could go a block over and buy a good coffee. Any time she needed one, she could just walk there. Until she had found the shop, she had no idea what good coffee tasted like. Now she was addicted. She headed over one last time, deciding she needed one for the trip back to Landstad.

It had taken almost the entire month, but she had come to the realization that she could live somewhere other than Landstad. She didn't love it here, but she saw the advantages that Anderson had loved about the place. She knew she had messed up, completely messed up, but she hadn't contacted him. In fairness, he didn't contact her either.

She had talked to her friends since they had two book club sessions while she was gone. The first time they had Facetimed the discussion, but it wasn't as much fun as usual. They had told her how mad Anderson had been when he found out she'd left. And that he had broken her door, or two doors, to be exact. It surprised her that she hadn't heard from the rental company about it, but Tess had confessed that she had told Anderson that Ruth owned the building. She had also told Ruth that Anderson that the door had been fixed by the end of the day.

The next time they got together, they had traveled to Grand Forks and met up with Ruth. It had been a lot better than the meeting before. Not as comfortable as her apartment in Landstad, but it had been nice to see familiar faces again. This time they said that Anderson was still there but that Rafferty was definitely working with him. Mia was keeping an eye on them for her.

It had now been a month, and so far, the girls had said Anderson was still in Landstad. She knew he was supposed to be out of the office by April first. That had passed, and she was tired of waiting for him to leave so that she could get back to her life. Or back to her apartment since her life was actually over.

Today she had decided it was time to leave. Today she would

confront Anderson if he was still in Landstad and tell him that she was willing to try living away from her home with him. If he wanted her, that was. It had been a month; he was most likely over her by now.

Opening the door to the coffee shop, she loved how the warm air and smell of coffee surrounded her when she stepped inside. It was like a hug when she really needed one. Walking to the counter, she smiled at the regular server who just wrote what she knew Ruth would ask for, and they chatted about the weather and things happening in the few blocks around them as Ruth paid and waited for her coffee. She had been surprised that she made friends in the big town. It had been far easier than she had ever suspected it would be.

Sylvia handed her the coffee, and Ruth headed out the door. She was almost to the door when she heard her name being called. Turning, she almost dropped her hot coffee cup when she saw Anderson coming towards her.

"Ruth, stop."

Why was he here? She needed the three-hour drive to figure out what she would say to him. Usually, it was a two-hour drive, but she was going to drive as slow as she could. She needed that time.

"Anderson." She breathed out his name. It felt foreign on her lips after the month of not saying it.

"I have been waiting here for two days. Waiting for you to come back," he said.

Not knowing what to say, she looked around as if someone else would have been looking for her here too. Did everyone know about her coffee shop addiction?

"Noel saw you here the other day, then she came back the next day and saw you again. She called me to tell me you were here," Anderson continued, but his words were not registering in her mind.

"Did the book club tell you where to find me?" she asked as he easily pulled her over to a table and sat her down. Nothing was making much sense. Anderson was there in person.

"Ruth?" was all he said, realizing she was not hearing him.

"Anderson," she answered, looking into his brown eyes.

"No, the book club didn't tell me, though I know that they've known for weeks. They kept your secret. Noel saw you last week, then again two days ago. She called me to tell me you were here, or at least that you came in here. I have been sitting here waiting for you to come back."

"I didn't come in yesterday," she replied as the story became clearer to her. It was still a shock that he was sitting in front of her. He had been waiting for her, here? He wanted to see her enough to wait for her?

"I know. I was waiting for you."

"Oh, yeah, you said that." Ruth wrapped her hands around her coffee in front of her.

"We need to talk. I know that you own the office building, Ruth. Why didn't you tell me?" He wrapped his hands over hers.

"I really didn't try to hide it from you. Well, yes, I did. I didn't want you to know that I owned it in the beginning. I didn't know you; you could have taken advantage of me. Later, I guess I enjoyed having something over you. Not after we got together, before that. Afterward, I was nervous and thought you would be mad at me for hiding it. You were mad that I didn't tell you I lived upstairs." She bit her lip. Had she said too much already?

"I would have understood. How long have you owned it?"

"Frank offered me the building at a low rate before he put the insurance office up for sale. He didn't get as much for the company without the building, but Frank always liked me and felt he owed me something for how Franky had treated me. He didn't, but I jumped at the chance to own the building."

"How did you have enough money for it?"

"I told you that I was to work and save money for when Franky came back. Well, I did that, even after Franky didn't come back. Frank didn't charge rent, utilities, or anything. I had almost no bills. I banked that money for years. I paid cash for the building."

"You had that kind of money just sitting around?"

"Yes. Then I looked around and saw so many other sad buildings for sale in town, and I bought them too. I fix them a little at a time so that they are good places to live and work. I want people to be happy when they live in town." It made her happy when people wanted to rent downtown, her downtown. Based on how easily she got people to rent from her, she knew they liked it as much as she did.

"Was that all money saved from working or was some of it book money?" he asked.

"Most was book money for the other buildings. I do well with that. Some of that money I have invested in the stock market and have done okay with it too." She smiled at her good fortune.

"Rafferty says that you give money to anyone who comes to the office looking for a donation," Anderson said.

"Yes, I don't need the money. When the high school needs money for prom or new uniforms, I am happy to help. When a local family needs some help, I help. I was there once, right in that community. There was more than one fundraiser to keep me alive before my transplant," she explained. She hoped that he would understand; not everyone would.

"I've missed you at the office," Anderson admitted.

"You have Rafferty now." Her heart broke at the words. She still wasn't ready to work with Rafferty, no matter how nice he could be to her. There was still pain there.

"Rafferty may be your brother, but he is not you, Ruth. Also, he never blushes over dirty words at your desk. Nor does he ever slip his shoes off under the desk." Anderson squeezed her hands.

"I have decided I am not going back to the office, Anderson." She pulled her hands from under his. "I don't want to be a personal assistant anymore. Instead, I want to focus on my writing for once."

"You're not coming back?" He sounded disappointed, and she knew he was.

"Not to the office. I am going back to live there today. The car is packed and ready to go. When do you leave?" It hurt to ask. That's why she had run away a month ago, to not see him leave her. And now it seemed she would be forced to once again be left behind anyway.

"Leaving has been the last thing on my mind. All I have been doing is looking for you. I haven't even thought about leaving," he admitted.

"But you are still leaving?" She asked, even if she knew the answer. He was always going to leave.

"Landstad was always a stepping stone to getting my own office. My dad is now seeing me as ready for more responsibility now. I would get my own office and even have agents under me. Not just one, but three or four. Since I started working for my dad, this has been my dream," he explained, something she should have listened to before running from town.

"You are going to love it there. Or here, I guess." She looked around the coffee shop, because this was the town he was going to be in. "You deserve the life you have always dreamed of."

"Your dreams are important also, Ruth. And You love Landstad, always have and always will. It's where you belong." He said with a sad smile.

"I decided I would rather be anywhere with you than in Landstad without you. I can write anywhere, but you are going to be here. I messed up by leaving, when I should have stayed and talked to you, but I don't do confrontation well. I love you, Anderson." She didn't turn to him.

The silence across from her finally made her turn and look at him. His eyes were on her, but she couldn't tell what he was thinking. She had laid it all out for him, and he was silent. He didn't want her back.

"I tried not to love you because I knew it would end, and I didn't want to be destroyed again. I have given my heart to two men, and neither has wanted it. When will I learn?" Pushing herself out of the booth, her coffee was left forgotten as she rushed out the door. Once free of the building, she did something she hadn't done in years: she really ran away.

Her only goal was to get to her car before the tears filled her eyes and she couldn't see. Now she had told him everything, and he didn't want her anymore. She had messed it all up. He had stopped loving her, just like Franky had years before.

The parking lot was in front of her, but she couldn't really see it through her tears.

Slowing to a stop, she leaned against a building and slid to the ground. Sitting with her back to the building, she wiped the tears away and saw her car. She had almost made it. Hugging her legs to her chest, she cried.

Anderson's voice came from somewhere near her. "Ruth, don't cry."

"Leave me alone," she said between sobs.

"No, Ruth, I am never leaving you alone again." He pulled her into his arms.

"You don't love me anymore. I destroyed that by leaving."

"No, you made me realize how much I really loved you by running. You showed me how much I love you in my life, just as it was. I loved the life we had together." He kissed her hair.

"But I lied to you about so much." She wiped away her tears again.

"You did. A few months ago, you were just a personal assistant that I didn't really notice. Now you are a business owner and a successful author. You have a cocky brother and a great group of overprotective friends. And you are funny and sexy, and I love to spend time with you. I just love you, Ruth." He kissed her wet cheek. "Even when you left that morning, I wanted to change you. I wanted you to fit into my world. I realized almost too late that I should have been trying to fit into your world."

"I can move, Anderson. I can live here. As long as you're here too," she insisted, not wanting that to be what stood between them. Not anymore.

"No, we will stay there. I don't need to have my own branch in Grand Forks. I have my own branch in Landstad. Now I have an agent under me, so I get to be a boss. I want you to be happy, and you will be happy in your apartment. And at the end of the day, I will get to see you there." He held her tighter.

"But you want more. You want the fancy job and the big house," she argued.

"Ruth, you changed my normal. I just want to be with you. One day we might move to a house in Landstad. I hear you already own a few. Until then, we will enjoy the downtown life and all it has to offer us."

"Are you sure? I don't want to be the reason you hate what you do or where you are. I don't want you to hate me."

"I will never hate you, Ruth Kennedy. I love you. And if I start hating it, we will look for something different. But talk to me, promise me you won't run away. I promise to talk to you if you promise to talk to me." He kissed her again.

"Promise," she whispered as his lips touched hers.

CHAPTER 25

As she followed Anderson down the stairs from their apartment, she couldn't stop smiling or watching his butt. Once at the ground level, he held the door for her to go through, and as she did, he lightly slapped her butt. "Stop looking at my butt, woman."

She laughed, surprised the morning was so warm for early May. Usually, the mornings were chilly, but today promised to be a warm day.

They slowly walked the few steps to the office, and he waited as she unlocked the door. Once she had it open, he pulled her into his arms, and it made her laugh until his mouth closed over hers. The kiss was a little too steamy for Main Street, and she heard Rafferty yelling about them getting a room from across the street. She ignored him and focused on Anderson.

Lifting his head, he kissed her nose before letting her go. "See you at lunch." Then he was gone, walking away from her across the quiet street where Rafferty was waiting on the sidewalk.

It had only been a month and a half since she had returned to Landstad. Just a short amount of time, but so much had happened already. For one, he had officially moved in. After spending a few weeks picking and choosing whose stuff stays and whose goes, they got rid of it all and started anew. Some of the stuff that was too nice to throw out had been moved into her office apartment. Most had been sold or set out for the garbage collectors or quick neighbors who beat the garbage collectors. Now it felt like home to both of them.

Once that was done, Anderson had decided that he and Rafferty should move their office back to Rafferty's building. It was bigger and had a better layout than Anderson's office, especially for two agents. So, they had worked to get that office set up. Rafferty hadn't even commented when Ruth had set up the network and all the computer equipment.

With a smile, she pushed into the office she had worked at for so many years. The new sign would come soon. When Anderson had suggested that she use the office as a base for her rental business, it had taken her a few days to realize it was a good idea. Why pay someone else to do her rental stuff when she could do it?

Sitting down at her old desk, she logged into the computer and waited for it to come alive. Out the window, she saw cars driving by and people milling around. It was a nice, almost summer day in North Dakota, so people were going to be outside.

Looking through some of the programs on the screen, she smiled and got up. The rental business was really not going to take any of her time, way less than even her secretary job had taken except on the first of the month, when the checks were mostly hand-delivered now. It was still a good day.

Leaving her old office area, she went into what was once Anderson's office. Now it resembled her office upstairs. Both her computers were set up, and the wall of computer equipment was all there, making the room cozy. Shutting the door behind her, she slipped off the sweater she had worn downstairs that morning. Hanging it on the back of the chair, she sat down and booted up the computer in front of her. Then she spun around and booted up the one behind her as well.

As they came to life, she slipped her headphones on her head. Looking through her phone for a playlist to listen to, she leaned back in her chair. It had been Anderson's idea to have her writing office down here so that she could still be a part of the community. It had turned out to be perfect. Not that she got many visitors, but she still felt like she knew what was happening in Landstad.

It had just been a week since she had been set up, and so far, it worked out great. Anderson would bring her lunch every day so that she ate, and she usually had one guest a day in for a chat. Sometimes it was Mia, and sometimes it was Tess. Sometimes it was just a high schooler looking for a donation. But still, it was people.

Most were offered a coffee from her new high-tech coffee machine. It was her first purchase for her office after coming back. It was a luxury from her time in the city she wasn't ready to give up, not just yet.

Computers up, she turned on the programs she wanted for the day and hit 'play' on her music, turning up the volume to block out except the phone, which would stop the music automatically for her. After reading a few sentences, she started to type.

OLIVER'S FINGERS skimmed over Grace's naked breasts, causing her breath to hitch. As his lips followed the same path as his fingers had gone, Grace's entire body throbbed.

Needing to feel his skin against hers, she worked the buttons on his crisp white shirt, her fingers shaky as his lips and tongue didn't let up on her nipples. Still tearing at the shirt, she moaned Anderson's name.

SMILING, she deleted out 'Anderson's name,' like always. He always ended up in her books, and sometimes she didn't even notice until the read-through. Having no idea how long she had been working, she nearly jumped when she saw the door swing open. A smile spread across her lips when she saw Anderson standing in the doorway. He hadn't brought lunch, which was odd.

Slipping the headphones off her head, she turned all her attention to him. "What are you doing here, handsome?"

He walked further into the room and said, "Just needed to see you. I miss seeing you all day."

Pushing her out of her chair and into his arms, she replied, "I miss you too."

"No, you don't, you don't even notice I am not here." He kissed her neck. Him kissing her in the office was easy to get used to.

"Sometimes I do." He was starting to see how engrossed she got in her work. Many days he stopped by the office on his way home, just to get her away from the computer. Otherwise, she would never come home.

"I love you, Ruth," he said, kissing down from her neck to the buttons of her shirt.

"I love you too, Anderson, but I am at work. It's professional space here." Pulling out of his arms, she walked to the door that separated the front office from the back office. A shiver ran through her, sensing that he was following to leave the professional space and go somewhere more private. Luckily, it was still just a few steps away and up a flight of stairs. So close.

But at the door, she stopped and decided to shut it, then turned to lean against it, locking it behind her. "But this is now *my* office, and everything is allowed in my office."

His arms went to either side of her, and she found herself trapped against the door. His mouth went back to her chest as her arms slip up to get his suit jacket off. Once it had slid to the floor, she pulled his shirt from his pants so that her hands could touch his warm skin, exactly what she'd wanted to do since she'd noticed him in her office.

His hands had started to undo the buttons she had buttoned up not that long ago. "I have wanted you in this office for months."

"I wrote about this years ago, so you are way behind. I hope it's as good in reality," she whispered.

"So much pressure, Ruth."

"I think you're up to it."

Her shirt fluttered to the floor, and his hands went to release her breasts from the dark red bra that held them in. "On the desk or here?"

"Here, the desk is too far away." She replied quickly, not wanting to wait as long as the five steps would take.

"I love you, Ruth Kennedy," he said as his lips finally kissed hers. She would have said those words too, but her mouth was too busy for a long time.

Behind her back a loud pounding shook the door, making Ruth groan in something other than pleasure. Who was so desperate to see her they would interrupt this important moment? Office sex that she had been wanting for what seemed like forever.

After the door knob moved, but since she and Anderson were leaning against it, the door didn't move. It didn't matter because Mia through the door yelled, "Ruth, we have an emergency, it's Tess. I need a master story teller for this.

Meeting Anderson's eyes, she cleared her throat and tried to sound normal, "Can it wait?"

"No, we have to get the gossip started now. I need your help." Mia admitted, and Ruth wished she could see her face when she admitted it.

"One minute." She promised as her she met Anderson's smile.

"Your friends need you, Ruth." He said, and brushed his thumb over her cheek.

He was right. Once upon a time, not that long ago, Mia would never have thought of asking Ruth anything. Now she was in her office asking for help, or maybe it was more like demanding. If there was anything that would make her leave Anderson right now it was to help her friends.

"We will continue this later." She promised as she pushed him away and straightened her clothes, hoping Mia didn't realize what they were doing.

"I will hold you to that promise." Anderson winked as he opened the door to let Mia rush inside, already talking about what trouble Tess had gotten into today. It didn't matter, she was there for whatever it was. Always.

EPILOGUE

"Ruth, we have a blowout!" Anderson yelled from the main apartment. Ruth was in her former office, now turned master bedroom with its own bathroom and small kitchenette. It was handy for when she didn't want to go far for coffee, which was a much-needed thing in the Miles house with two little girls under the age of two.

"Just clean her up!" she yelled back. She only had a few minutes to get the bedroom clean before Kim and Dan arrived. They were frequent guests since Mary Elizabeth had been born within a year after Mary Margaret, or Eliza and Maggie. Now his parents were regular visitors.

"It's too much." His voice was getting closer, which meant he was not going to the baby's actual room. He was heading her way.

When he appeared in the doorway, he was holding a smiling, happy nine-month-old under the armpits, as far from him as possible. It was still his usual stance when in the situation. Despite all that, the little girl was adorable with her dad's dark hair and dark eyes. Neither one of her kids had inherited her blonde hair, and for that, Ruth was happy.

"Anderson, you have to take care of it. I am trying to get this place to look like we don't have kids. I don't need your parents knowing that I don't actually like to clean. Since they already know I don't like to cook, I need them to believe I do something around here." She tossed another handful of clothes into the laundry basket before kicking it into the closet and shutting the door.

After Maggie had been born, Anderson had insisted that they make the storage apartment into their bedroom. Though it had seemed odd at the time, after getting new carpet and updating the bathroom, it had turned out perfect. They had left the little kitchen, just fixed it up a little—who knew how handy that would be in their bedroom? With the remodel of her writing apartment, they had redesigned the hallway between the apartments, giving them a new door and an actual place to store their jackets and boots.

"If you help me, I will help you."

"If you take care of that, I will not need help."

"Please, wife," Anderson begged.

Yes, she had married him. After living with him in sin and having a child with him out of wedlock, she had made an honest man out of him and married him. At that time, she was pregnant again, and once the novelty of being talked about around town had worn off, they had gotten married in front of all their friends and family. Or actually, they'd gotten remarried since they had already secretly gotten married when she had found out she was pregnant the first time. Her need to not repeat her mom's mistakes was too high, and she had panicked for a moment, so they had gone to Vegas on a weekend without the town knowing it had even happened. Once home, they hadn't told a soul, and she had started to enjoy the whispers.

So, the second wedding had been all for show and their parents. Then they had gone on a long-week honeymoon, leaving Eliza with Dan and Kim. For a while she had felt guilty, that was until they upped their visits tenfold after. They only stayed a few hours when they visited, but since she and Anderson didn't have room, and there was no hotel in town, a few hours felt long when it was so often.

Added to that, Sara had not wanted to be shown up by Anderson's parents, so she started taking Eliza as often as possible, including just after her first birthday for a week. So, she and Anderson had gone on a vacation that had brought them Maggie nine months later.

"We switch jobs, and I will take the girls to my parents' next weekend. You stay here and write." Anderson sounded desperate with the baby still dangling from his arms.

"Deal!" she yelped. No way was she letting that offer slip by her for a little baby poop. Grabbing the kid from him with a smile, she walked back into her once spotless apartment. It seemed that Eliza was up and not into keeping the apartment clean, so it was less-than-spotless now.

To say that her writing had been affected by having kids was an understatement. She was releasing about three books a year and was getting closer to two. But she was raising Anderson's babies, and that was more important. A weekend to herself, however, was a dream come true.

Quickly, she changed the baby and got her into a new outfit. Walking out of the room, she saw that her in-laws were there and were already hugging on Eliza, who was happy to be the center of attention. With a happy greeting, she handed the baby to them.

"How are you feeling, Ruth?" Kim asked, taking the baby from her.

"Like a woman who should know how not to get pregnant after having two kids so close." She patted her stomach, which was showing that she was four months pregnant, not that she was hiding it. But sometimes it was hard to be the woman with kids so close in age, and she was well into her thirties.

"I read your latest release; it is no wonder you got pregnant." Her mother-in-law had turned into her biggest fan, which was awkward for Ruth, who wrote way too many books about the woman's son. So far, she hadn't said anything about that.

The rest of the town had also turned into avid fans since word got out that she was a writer. Now, besides running her rentals from her office, she had to keep copies of her books to sell. Even though she made money with every sale, it was starting to cut into her writing time, enough to where she was thinking about hiring a personal assistant of her own.

"Those are fiction, Kim," Ruth reminded her, as always.

"Of course, dear. I can't see you and Andy having sex in a hotel pool after it was closed for the night. It is all made up, but you do have quite the imagination." Kim recapped a scene from the book that Ruth had released two months before.

Ruth caught Anderson's eye across the room, and he winked at her face turning red in embarrassment. The baby she was carrying might've been the product of that scene, including the forgotten condom and the near-drowning that took place afterward.

Thankfully, her mother-in-law didn't notice as Ruth turned and hurried into the kitchen, leaving the older couple with the kids. Anderson joined her, kissed her forehead, and caressed her obvious baby bump. Then he whispered, "I loved that scene also. Almost as much as I loved putting it in your imagination."

Pushing him away, she hissed, "Shut up, or I will tell her it was all your idea."

Grabbing her back, he pulled her to him, pressing his body into hers. "One of my best, right after seducing my personal assistant. Though without the one, there wouldn't be the other."

"You know, it was four years ago today that you kissed me in the stairway after getting me drunk." She watched Kim and Dan playing with the girls; she loved seeing how much they adored their grandkids.

"Today, huh? Then I think we'll have to celebrate tonight. I already have something in mind that we should try. Something for your next book." He kissed her neck.

"What?" she asked skeptically.

"If I told you, you wouldn't have nearly as much fun. Besides, I have to inspire my romance writer; keep her guessing." He pulled her even tighter to him and ran his hand over her barely showing belly.

"You, Anderson, are all the inspiration I need."

THE END

ALSO BY ALIE GARNETT

<u>Landstad, ND</u>

<u>Invisible</u>

<u>Irresistible</u>

<u>Impulsive</u>

<u>Insuppressible</u>

<u>Intriguing</u>

<u>Imperfect</u>

<u>Irreplaceable</u>

<u>The Great Lovely Falls</u>

Falling for the Single Mom

Falling for his Best Friends Sister

Falling for the Boss

Falling for his Step-Sister

Falling for his Fake Wife

Falling into a Second Chance

<u>Hart Series</u>

Seeing her Pain

Her Favor

Max Valentine is Looking at Me!

Keeping her Safe

<u>Stand Alone</u>

Romancing the Doctor